now that you're here

DUPLEXITY, PART I

Coming Soon

DUPLEXITY, PART II
while you were gone

now that you're here

DUPLEXITY, PART I

AMY K. NICHOLS

ALFRED A. KNOPF   NEW YORK

THIS IS A BORZOI BOOK PUBLISHED BY ALFRED A. KNOPF

Visit us on the Web! randomhouseteens.com

Educators and librarians, for a variety of teaching tools, visit us at RHTeachersLibrarians.com

Library of Congress Cataloging-in-Publication Data
Nichols, Amy.
Now that you're here / Amy K. Nichols.—First edition.
p. cm.—(Duplexity ; part 1)
Summary: When a street-smart graffiti artist, Danny, is jolted into a parallel world, only Eevee, an alluring science geek, has the know-how to get him home. But as he falls for her, he isn't so sure home is where he wants to be.
ISBN 978-0-385-75389-0 (trade)—ISBN 978-0-385-75391-3 (ebook)
ISBN 978-0-385-75396-8 (pbk.)
[1. Space and time—Fiction. 2. Identity—Fiction. 3. Graffiti—Fiction. 4. Artists—Fiction. 5. Science fiction.] I. Title.
PZ7.N527Now 2014   [Fic]—dc23   2013044494

The text of this book is set in 11.5-point Requiem.

Printed in the United States of America
December 2014
10 9 8 7 6 5 4 3 2 1

First Edition

FOR JIM

walk forever by my side

1

EEVEE

There are two basic principles in chaos theory. The first is that every system has an underlying order, regardless of its complexity. The second is that even the smallest variance in a system can cause seemingly unrelated behaviors or events.

A butterfly in the Congo flaps its wings and causes rain to fall in Belgium.

A boy shows up at my door and sets off a series of events that shatters everything I understand about the universe.

And my place in it.

2

Danny

Germ parks under a tree in front of Frankie's Fritters and kills the engine. "Here we are, Ogden." He leans forward to peer out the windshield, his hands still gripping the steering wheel. "The last gig."

I look out the passenger window. People gather along Port Royale Way, setting up blankets and chairs. Beyond them, cars stream into the mall parking lot. "The Patriot Day parade? Really?"

"You saw the instructions."

"Yeah, but why? So many people."

Germ shrugs. "They want to get their message out?"

"Or they want us to get caught." I crane my neck to look through the back window. Compliance officers must be patrolling. Unless they're going solely Spectrum, but that's not likely. Too late to back out now. Just need to get it over with and be done. "We'll have to work quick. Stay out of sight." I point down the road. "I've got from ShopMart to the gallery."

"I'm on the other side," Germ says. "Fifth Avenue Fashion around to Mission Tire."

"All right. Let's do this."

We bump fists, grab our skateboards and bags and head out, covering our faces to avoid cameras. At least it's cloudy. Low light and shadows help confuse the facial recognition.

Germ skates north, and I go south, my board rumbling over the asphalt as I weave between parked cars and people. Last month the target was the Del Mar Country Club. The month before, Phoenix Harbor Supply. Always a different location, but the job stays the same: paint symbols on the sides of buildings and don't get caught.

We used to only do random drops. Courier underground goods from one person to another, or pass memory sticks along an information route. For those, we never take money. It's cool just doing something to help. Like, maybe there's information about someone's family on that drive you're carrying. Most times, though, we're in it for the dosh. Doesn't pay much. Just enough to buy paint.

But then we got recruited to do bigger jobs. During a routine drop at a market house, this old lady handed us a letter saying street artists were needed to paint the city. So of course we signed up.

The agreement was simple. Pick up the stencils and directions, do the job, return the stencils, get paid. No big.

Until we put two and two together and figured out it was Red December calling the shots. Then we backed off. I mean, I hate the system as much as anyone, but you'd have to be crazy to get involved with those kinds of extremists. I'm through risking my neck. After today, we're done.

I skate around to the far side of the strip mall, away from the crowds, and crouch between two cars. Rest my back against the chain-link fence. Behind me is the service road. A woman stands at the back door of the beauty-supply store, risking an illicit smoke. She takes a drag, looks around, takes another.

A car passes and I crouch lower. Make sure I'm hidden. A second woman pops her head out of the door and the two talk. Come. *On.*

Finally, the smoker crushes the tip of the cigarette into the metal door, brushes away the ash with her hand and tucks the butt into the cuff of her jeans. The door closes behind them and I'm in business.

Two cans of red and my shirt pulled up over my nose, I go to town. Work my way across the strip mall, moving like a ninja, spraying the stencils about twenty feet apart. Same bunch of nonsense. Crown. Cockroach. Skull. Rocket. And a new one: mushroom. Clearly, it's some kind of code, but hell if I know what it means. That's someone else's job. If I had my way, this wall would be covered in real art.

When I reach the end of the building, the paint nozzle gums up for the millionth time. I pick at it with my fingers and teeth until it finally comes clean. My hands and shirt are covered in red. The acrid smell of paint hangs in the air.

The rumble of an engine stops me, and I duck behind a dumpster in time to avoid a patrol car. The camera on its roof trolls for baddies. I tug my hood down lower, just in case, and try to blend in with the shadows. The car slows almost to a stop, then pulls away. There's no way he didn't see the symbols. I look at the wall, and check the stencils in my hands. Didn't get the last one up. Oh well. Too bad, Red December. I'm out of here. I stuff the junked-up cans into my backpack and take off for Frankie's.

That took way longer than it should have. Germ's probably sitting there waiting for me.

Back on the main road, people line the street, filling the sidewalks and spilling over into the parking areas. Events like this are always the same: everyone wants to be seen, everyone has to make sure it's clear they're on the right side. I pop my board up into my hands and walk. Best to try and blend in. Music carries over the crowd from the PA system, that song we learned in third grade. *Something-something we will stand, for brother, sister, motherland.* I keep my guilty hands in my pockets as I wind through people and picnics and children chasing each other and stabbing their little flags like swords.

Just as the Frankie's sign comes into view, the music cuts to the jarring blare of a siren. Everyone freezes and listens. Flags are dropped as hands cover ears. From the speakers, an automated female voice says, "This is an evacuation notice. Proceed to the closest secure zone in a calm manner. This is an evacuation . . ."

I have to get to Frankie's. Have to find Germ.

The wheels of my board slap the blacktop and I push off, trying to weave through the crowd as the happy carnival turns to chaos. Everyone clambers for escape.

Maybe going the long way around the back of the stores will be quicker? I dart between the dry cleaner's and the bike shop, back to where I was working.

The fence. Damn. Forgot about the fence. I'll have to brave the crowds.

I do a 180 and slam to a stop. A security guard in a golf cart blocks my path. Our eyes meet and everything slows. He's big. Mean-looking. Cold spreads across my shoulders, down my arms. I blink first, and like *that* he's after me, yelling into his radio.

I whip around again and skate hard for the fence. On the other side is freedom. My hood flies off. There's no dodging Spectrum now. I aim for the dumpster at the far end. Just before I face-plant into the metal, I pop the board up, smack all four wheels against the dumpster's side and launch myself at the chain links. My fingers make contact, gripping the metal while my feet search for a hold. The guard's right behind me, reaching for me. My feet slip down again. I'm not gonna make it—

The first explosion shakes the ground, rattles the fence, blows out my eardrums. The security guard stumbles back and falls. My fingers scrape the metal, trying to hang on. Smoke engulfs the sky.

The second explosion crashes through me, pins me to the fence, squeezes the air from my lungs. Then suddenly, somehow, I'm flying. Blinding white heat swallows me, spits me out, slams me to the pavement. Pain explodes in my chest. I crumple as the ground gives way and I'm falling through, my legs kicking at nothing but dark, empty.

3

EEVEE

Numbers are safe. One is one is one. One will never be two. One will never be one thousand. Numbers don't change, which is why I like them. It's also why I like Warren. Not *like* like. But it's why we're friends. He doesn't change. With Warren, I know what to expect. I think he'd say the same about me, too. He knows I'm not going to play the drama queen or go girl psycho on him.

"I'm leaning toward the long-term effects of gamma radiation exposure." Warren swaps out his history book for calc.

The mirror inside my locker catches the reflection of Stacy Farley (cheerleader, blond, perfect) flirting with Justin Campbell (footballer, tall, dumb as a box of rocks). When they start kissing, I grab English and close the locker door. "I think we're better off doing something more tangible. Like Phoenix temperature variances over the last hundred years."

"Solomon," Warren groans, "Moon Mountain AP ran that one last year."

"I thought it sounded familiar."

I squint against the sunlight as we leave the locker bay. It's a perfect morning, and students crowd the sidewalks winding around the buildings of Palo Brea's open campus. Warren and I navigate our way through the best we can. An upperclassman bumps into Warren and growls, "Move it, bug-eyes."

Warren shrugs it off and adjusts his ever-present goggles. "Consequences of illegal dumping on desert ecology?"

"No animals."

"Effects of climate change on the migration patterns of the monarch—"

"I said no animals. Bugs are animals."

"You're making this really difficult."

"The deadline for the science fair is over a month away." I step aside to allow a gaggle of goths to slink past. "We've got time."

"It'll be here before we know it. And this year we actually stand a chance of winning. *If* we can come up with a killer idea. Mac said so."

"We have time. We'll figure it out."

"What, like the idea's just going to drop out of the sky?"

"You never know."

"Asteroids." Warren looks up. "Improved detection and tracking methods of Potentially Hazardous Asteroids."

"Too big. And we'd have to partner with NASA or something."

He shrugs. "We have Mac."

We've reached the fork in the sidewalk. Math building to the east, English to the west.

"Hi, Warren." Missy Bivins holds her books across her chest and her braids sway with each step.

Warren blushes. "Hey, Missy."

"See you in math."

We've been going to school with her since forever, but she and Warren never seemed to notice each other. Until this year. Now whenever she comes around, he loses his ability to speak. Or reason. I clear my throat.

"Huh?" He blinks. "Oh, where were we? Bugs—no, asteroids!"

"How about we take this up again after school?"

"It's Friday. Chess club."

The bell rings.

"Tonight," he says. "Cheese crisps up on the roof."

"Can't. Mom's taking me to the ballet. Geocaching tomorrow?"

"Make it so." He holds up his hand in the Spock sign. "Live long and prosper."

I meander to English, timing my arrival for just after second bell. No one hurries to Ms. Fischbach's—The Fish's—class. Most students linger outside and slip in just before the last bell. Some come in late just to tick her off. Long before I got to Palo Brea High, someone scratched BEWARE THE FISH into the paint, right at eye level. Janitors are always spackling over it, but the next day it's back—like a virus. The Fish hates it, which makes it all the more brilliant.

I wait for a few more people to show up before following them inside, keeping my eyes down and slinking through the aisles to my desk. Far right, near the back.

The Fish uses an alphabetical seating chart. She thinks, even as sophomores, we're not mature enough to handle sitting where we want. A-to-Z puts me behind Sarah Ranston and in front of Kyle Stiplar. Sarah wears too much perfume and flips her hair around so that her stink puffs up in my face. Kyle insists on putting his feet on the bar under my chair and he never stops moving. My only consolations: the wall on my right, and Danny Ogden on my left.

Danny is like another wall. He never moves or says anything. Just sits like a lump, with his head down and his moppish hair draping over his arms.

I pull out my notebook, open to the English section and continue the box fractal I'd started in class on Wednesday. Sarah flips her hair onto my desk and my pen slips, scratching a line in the wrong direction and ruining the symmetry. I clear my throat and push against her chair to scoot myself away. Kyle's feet push back. I'm trapped.

The late bell rings and The Fish rises from her desk. She's wearing the purple jumpsuit with the zipper running up over her bulging belly. The green scarf around her neck and the scowl on her face make her look like an angry eggplant.

"An update, to begin with," she says, holding up the baby book. The class gives a silent-but-visible groan. Ever since The Fish learned she was having a baby, she's taken every opportunity to turn the pregnancy into a teachable moment. Never mind she teaches English, not science. Never mind it grosses us all out. "This is week twenty-eight. Our baby is fourteen inches long and weighs approximately three pounds."

The door opens and Danny trudges into the room, his high-tops squeaking against the linoleum. The Fish watches him sit down. If her eyes could shoot lasers, Danny Ogden would be fried.

"Her eyelashes are developing, and if she were a boy, her testes would start descending."

This time the groan is audible. The guys sink down into their desks. Danny lays his head on his.

A voice pipes up from the back. "Maybe she'll have 'em anyway." Shock ripples through the room as everyone searches out who dared to speak against The Fish. Brian Finney's arms are crossed over his chest and he's wearing a smug grin. Clearly, the idiot has a death wish. No one moves. Brian looks around, disappointed he didn't get a single laugh. "What? It happens sometimes. I saw it on TV."

The Fish snaps the book closed. "I will not be disrespected in my classroom, Mr. Finney. Out." Then she gasps, puts her hand over her stomach and takes several deep breaths.

Please go into labor. Go. Go now.

But The Fish's moment of drama passes as soon as the door shuts on Brian. "Turn to page 774 in your anthology," she says. "Randy, you may read aloud while I return last week's essays." She waddles up and down the rows, stopping at each desk to shuffle through the papers cradled in her arms. Poor Randy clears his throat and begins reading in a slow, stuttered dirge while the rest of us fantasize about being anywhere else.

"'An Experiment in M-m-misery,' by Stephen C-crane."

Sounds like a story about our class.

"'It w-w-was late at night, and a fine rain was s-swirling softly down, uh, causing the p-p-pavements to glisten with hue of s-s-steel and blue and y-y-yellow in the rays of the in-in-in—'"

"Innumerable." The Fish's voice snaps like a whip from the next row over, where she is dispensing marked-up essays among the *M*'s.

"'Innumerable lights. A y-youth was t-t-trudging slowly, without enth-th-uzzziasm, with his hands buried d-d-deep in his t-t-trousers pockets—'"

"That's enough, Randy." The Fish places my essay face-down on my desk. Randy looks relieved it's over. "Eve, you may continue where Randy left off."

Ugh. My turn. I trace the lines of text with my finger. "'Toward the downtown places where beds can be hired for coppers. He was clothed in an aged and tattered suit . . .'"

I continue to read, but my mind wanders to the essay on my desk. Will I have to rewrite this one, same as last time? I can hear Dad lecturing already.

"'He looked about him searching for an outcast of highest degree that they two might share miseries.'"

"Thank you, Eve. Michael, now you."

I tap Kyle's leg to get him to stop jiggling my chair. He grunts. I turn the essay over. Scrawled in perfect red hand-writing is a note:

> *While you finally seem to be getting a handle on grammar, you continue to insist on forcing literature into strict paradigms. Think beyond the confines of the story. Rewrite. Grade: D.*

Why can't short stories be like fractions or geometric puzzles? Clear, concise, absolute. Then it would have easily been an A. I slide the essay under my notebook and listen to Michael read. Soon his voice turns to blah-blah in my ears and my attention slips back to the box fractal. I try to fix the ruined spot, but the mistake line curves in a way that isn't mathematically correct. It bothers me, like a painting hanging crooked on a wall. I trace and retrace the curve, deepening it until it's closer to accurate. It resembles half of a heart. The pen slowly slices through the paper.

Out of nowhere, Danny gasps and bolts upright in his seat. Scares the crap out of me. The pen falls from my hand and rolls to the ground. He grips the desk, elbows locked, and raises his chin enough that his hair falls back from his face. He looks around the room, moving only his eyes.

"Nice of you to join us, Mr. Ogden," The Fish remarks, before turning to her next victim. She points a fat finger. "Amanda, please read."

Everyone returns to listening to the short story. Except me. I watch Danny from the corner of my eye. He relaxes a little, but still holds on to the desk, his knuckles white. I lean over and pick my pen up from the floor. When I sit up, his eyes meet mine and I freeze.

They're blue, saucer-like.

"You," he whispers.

Me? What did I do? I press myself into the arm of my chair, as far away from him as possible, and keep my eyes down on the notebook. Sarah's perfume chokes out all the oxygen in the room. My chair jiggles in a constant Kyle quake. And all the while, Danny won't stop staring at me.

I hear the sound of ripping paper, then a note lands near my left shoe. The idiot is going to get us both in trouble. I try to ignore it, the inch of badly folded white with the mystery message inside. What does it say? What does he want? When I can't stand not knowing any longer, I make sure The Fish's back is turned and reach down to pretend-scratch my leg. My fingers snatch the note and I sit up, hiding my hands behind Sarah's massive hair.

It's a simple question written in wobbly black capitals: *WHERE ARE WE?*

I scribble a single-word response: *Hell.* When The Fish turns away again, I toss the paper back over. Danny catches it one-handed. Pretty good reflexes for a stoner who spends most of his time asleep.

He crumples the note in his fist and opens his mouth to say something to me, but The Fish speaks first.

"Danny, you may pick up where Carson left off."

He looks around at everyone watching him.

Then he bolts from the room.

The door bangs shut. Through pursed lips, The Fish says, "Sarah, you read instead."

4

Danny

What. The.

The door bangs behind me and I run full force into blinding sunshine. My lungs feel like they're gonna explode, but I push forward, running through the parking lot and past the gates until I'm free.

And lost.

I turn in a slow circle, catching my breath, eyes watering from the sun. Where's the mall? The parade? The people?

My fingers fumble at the crumpled note still clutched in my hand.

WHERE ARE WE?

Hell.

I have to find Germ.

Dodging cars, I race across four lanes of traffic into a sprawling neighborhood. This isn't the Phoenix I know. The sun is too bright. The air too dry. Not a Spectrum cam to be seen. My legs feel like they're made of concrete. One foot catches the other and I go down. Knees slam the road. Pain rockets through me as I roll to my back and spit hair out of my mouth.

Hair? I stretch the long strands up toward the sky—eight inches of hair that weren't there this morning are now rooted to my head. Blood oozes where my hands scraped the road. Bits of red smudge the cuffs of a black leather jacket I've never seen before. My head falls back to the asphalt, jarring my teeth.

Get up, Ogden. Find Germ. Find Dad. Find someone.

My legs kick against the pain as I stumble through the streets, heading what should be south. If I keep going this way, I'll get to my neighborhood. If I can make it. My breathing goes ragged and I fall into a limp, the high-tops clomping. My lungs burn like I'm hauling, but I'm getting nowhere fast. The road turns and ends in a cul-de-sac.

Lost again. And no choice but to go back the way I came.

"All right, Danny," I mutter. "Keep it together, man."

I drag my ass back through the neighborhood, mumbling the things I recognize from the first pass. Garbage can. Blue house. Block wall. Gravel yard. Cactus. Barking dog. The sound of traffic rumbles ahead. Getting close. I stumble forward until finally I reach the main road.

Back where I started.

This time I wait for a break in traffic, then limp across the street and back onto campus, defeated. Nothing is right here. Everything is out of place. Maybe I'll find answers back at the school. Those people seemed to know me at least.

"Where's the office?" I ask a scrawny kid with glasses. My swollen lip bumbles the words.

He looks at me like he's afraid I'll pound him. Points to a building and darts off.

I push open the office door. The woman behind the desk gasps. "Oh my." She stands. "This way." We walk through a hallway lined with framed certificates and trophy cases. The smell of alcohol stings the air. I reach out and touch the wall to keep my balance.

"Clara?" the office lady says.

The nurse looks up from her snack. "What happened to you?" She snaps the lid over her food and gets to work. Sits me up on the exam table. Puts an ice pack on my head. Dabs goop on my lip and scrubs my hands with stinky orange soap.

"Did you get beat up again?"

Can't speak with the thermometer under my tongue, so I shake my head.

"Fall?"

I nod.

"Does it hurt anywhere? Ribs? Head?"

I point to my knee. She pushes up the jeans leg, which is so tight she can barely get it over my swollen knee. She feels the sides and back, moves the kneecap, bends and straightens the leg. Takes the thermometer from my mouth and reads it. Wipes it with alcohol and puts it in a glass container.

"I was running," I say. "I tripped."

She raises an eyebrow. Doesn't believe me.

I hold up a hand to show her the road rash. "Landed in the street."

"You were off campus?"

"Parking lot."

"Ah."

Definitely doesn't believe me.

She takes away the ice and examines the back of my head. "That's a big bump." She touches it and I wince. "Dizzy?"

"A little."

She flashes a penlight across my eyes.

"Follow my finger." She moves her hand back and forth in front of my face. "Squeeze my hands as hard as you can."

I squeeze and it's her turn to wince. She hands me the ice pack and I put it back on my head. I stare at my knees, compare their sizes. Bend my right leg, just to make sure the pain is still real.

It is.

"This is Clara Meeks, nurse at Palo Brea High School," she says into the phone. "Danny fell and got pretty banged up. I'm recommending he see a doctor. What time will you be here to pick him up?"

My heart's thumping. Who is she talking to?

"Thank you." She hangs up the phone. "Your ride will be out front. You're welcome to wait here. He said it will take a little while."

Must be Dad. Good. This is good.

The paper on the table crinkles as Nurse Clara helps me lie back. She sets an ice pack over my knee and adjusts the one under my head. A frozen pillow.

As the pain goes numb, the room feels like it's tilting and taking me with it. The pockmarks on the ceiling form patterns. Gnarly faces looking down. Dad will be here soon. We'll go home and everything will be okay. I listen to the sounds around me, the muted voices, the rhythm of a copy machine, the sound of my breathing. The spinning stills. My face relaxes, then my shoulders. My body sinks into the table like it weighs a—

"Oh no you don't." Nurse Clara's voice jerks me awake. "No falling asleep. Not with a bump like that on your noggin."

I blink against the lights. A headache blooms behind my eyes.

Office Lady knocks twice on the open door. "Danny's ride is waiting in the east lot."

"Thanks." Nurse Clara helps me sit up. "Want me to walk out with you?"

"No. I got it." I topple off the table and shuffle to the door. "Which way is east?"

She frowns, points. "See a doctor, Danny. And no more *falling down,* okay?"

I shake off the woozy feeling as I walk in the direction Nurse Clara pointed. My eyes search the lot, but I don't see Dad's car.

The reverse lights of a work truck parked at the curb blink on. The truck rolls backward and the equipment on the racks clatters. Then the truck stops. In front of me.

"You want me to carry you or something?" The voice is gruff. Angry.

I peer through the passenger window. Never seen the guy before. He's greasy. The cab stinks. "Ain't in the mood for your bull crap, Danny. Get your ass in the truck."

5

EEVEE

The clock on the dash reads 10:32 when Mom pulls into the driveway. I crane my neck to see if Warren's on his roof. He isn't. She turns off the engine and the car chimes to remind her to take her key out of the ignition. She yawns. "Where are you staying tonight?"

The light is on in Dad's front room next door. Awake and reading, no doubt. He'll ask how I did on my English essay. Mom, on the other hand, is too tired to care. "I'll stay here."

She pulls the key and the chiming stops. "Honey?"

My hand grips the passenger-door handle. Here comes the awkward. Ever since she turned forty and started seeing this New Agey life coach, things have been weird. She gave up accounting for real estate. Changed her hair and how she dresses. Began reading books like *How to Relate to Your Teen* and *101 Fun Mother-Daughter Dates*. Fashion magazines started showing up, too, left open to the style-guide pages. She drops hints about my hair and nails and clothes, like I should try harder to look like all the other fifteen-year-old girls out there. So what will it be this time? The fact that I wore jeans tonight instead of a dress?

She surprises me, though, with a simple "Thank you for going tonight. I know it's not your thing."

The truth is, I actually enjoyed the ballet. The precision of the dancers' movements timed to the music. The shapes and colors and rhythms changing and morphing. It was a perfect blend of art and physics. I can't tell her this, though. If I do, what would be next? A makeover? Charm school? So I answer, "You're welcome," and leave it at that.

We gather our things and walk toward the house. As I pass the garage, a figure steps from the shadows. "Eevee?"

I stumble back. "What are *you* doing here?"

Mom calls from near the front door, "Everything okay?" Then she sees Danny and her eyes just about pop out of her head. I can read on her face what she's thinking: *My daughter is talking to a boy!* She smiles. "Hello. Is this a friend of yours, Eve?"

"Mom, this is Danny," I say, keeping my distance from both of them. "He's from school."

She shuffles her bags. "Nice to meet you, Danny. I'm Judy."

He pushes his hair out of his eyes and shakes her hand. "Nice to meet you, too, Mrs. Solomon."

"It's Bennett, actually. Ms. Bennett." Mom smiles at me, then at Danny, then at me again. Now that she's had a closer look, she doesn't seem quite so sure about him. Still, she says in her chirpiest voice, "I'll leave you two to talk."

"No, it's okay. I'm coming inside."

She mouths, *Don't be rude* before making a big show of bustling off to the house. The door closes with a click and I'm alone with him.

"How do you know where I live?"

"I didn't. I followed you home from school earlier."

That's all I need to hear.

"Wait. Eevee."

"I don't know what this is about, but I don't want any part of it. Go away."

"Go where? I can't find anyone. You're the only link I have."

"Link to what? You don't even know me."

"But I thought after the museum and then seeing you today, you—"

"Go home, Danny." I open the front door.

"I can't."

Cold twists in my stomach and my legs feel like they're made of osmium. "Why not?"

"He took me to some house, but it wasn't mine. And I tried to find my house, but . . ." His voice trails off, and he mumbles, "Everything is wrong."

"Who took you? What happened?"

"I don't know," he says. "I'm not me. This. This isn't . . ." He motions at Mom's house, the street. "Where are we?"

"Phoenix? United States? Earth?"

He shakes his head. His eyes look desperate.

"Okay." I hold up my hands to try to calm him down. "Let's take this slow. You're Danny Ogden, right?"

"Right, but I'm—"

"Just yes or no."

"Yeah. In here." He touches his temple.

"You live in Phoenix."

"Right, but—"

"You're still in Phoenix."

"No," he says. "No. I was at the mall. And there was a huge explosion. I hit my head and next thing I knew I was in that class." He balls his fists over his eyes and shakes his head. "Oh God. What about Germ?"

I step toward him. "Danny, did you take something?"

"No. I was—" He holds his right hand out, palm up. "I was there." He flips it over. "And then I was here." He looks up. "This can't be Phoenix. What about Spectrum?"

I shake my head.

"Cameras? Compliance? Where is all of that?" He wipes a hand over his face. "You have to believe me. I have no idea how I ended up in that classroom."

"You walked in late, just like you do every day." The events replay in my mind. "Then you fell asleep, like you do every day. And then you ran out, which I have to admit was something new."

"Right!" He points at me with both hands. "I ran into the neighborhood, but I got lost. So I went back to the school. To the nurse. She called someone and this guy showed up, and he drove me to a house and dropped me off. He told me not to let this happen again."

"Let what happen?"

"Make him leave work? I don't know. He was pissed. Really pissed." He moves the hair out of his face and I see the swollen purple skin under his eye.

"Then he opened the truck door like nothing happened and drove off."

"What did you do?"

"I found a key in my pocket that fit the lock." He takes a step toward me. "Eevee, I've never seen that house before. Whoever those people are, they aren't my parents."

"Why did you go in?"

"I thought maybe there'd be some answers in there. And I was starving." He tucks his hands in his pockets. "There were pictures on the fridge. One was of me." He swallows hard. "I think it's a foster home."

I don't know what to say. He really seems to be in trouble, but what can I do to help? All I come up with is, "That's really strange."

"It doesn't make sense. I live with my parents. Always have."

"You said you tried to find your house?"

He nods. "I wandered around, but everything is so different. I got lost and didn't know what to do. I went back to the school and hung around until I saw you leaving. After I knew where you lived, I made it my home base. I tried to find my house, but I couldn't. By the time I got back here, you were gone."

"You could have said something to me at school."

He looks away. "I was scared, I guess."

"Of me?" I laugh.

"I wasn't sure what you . . . you know . . . thought of me. After."

Clearly, I've missed something. "After what?"

"The museum."

I shake my head and he looks at me like I'm the crazy one. He reaches into his back pocket. "I kept the brochure." But instead of a brochure, he pulls out a wallet and turns it over in his hands. "This isn't mine." He crouches down and dumps out the contents on the grass.

Mom sticks her head out the door, startling both of us. "You two need anything?" She sees Danny sorting through the odds and ends, and whispers, "Is he okay?"

"He's having problems at home," I whisper back.

"What kind of problems?" We watch him mumbling to himself.

"He's scared."

"Of?"

I try to make my face convey the obvious. When Mom doesn't get my drift, I say, "I don't think it's safe for him to go back there."

"Oh?" she says. Danny looks up at us. His bruised eye appears even worse from this angle.

"Oh," she says again, but this time it's in surprise. Then her face changes to resolute. "Take him next door. He'll stay there tonight. I'll call your father to let him know."

I turn so Danny can't see me, and mouth, *Are you crazy?*

"It'll be okay." She motions me toward him. "Go."

She is crazy. She's completely lost her mind this time.

I take several steps backward, still making a face at her, then turn when I get close to Danny. "Come on. We're going to my dad's." He stuffs crumpled money and ID cards into his pockets, and we walk together through the shadows that crisscross the driveway.

"Your dad lives next door?"

"It's a long story," I mutter.

6

Danny

Over at her dad's place, she reaches for the door, but I stop her. "You believe me, right?"

"I don't know what to think," she says. "But I do know you shouldn't have to stay where people give you black eyes."

She knocks twice and opens the door. I follow her inside. The place is spotless. Like a picture from a magazine. Leather couch and chairs. Glass coffee table. Bookshelves lined with hardcovers. Her dad sits in the far corner under a reading lamp. Thinning hair. Glasses. He stands when he sees me. He wears slippers with business casual.

"Dad?" Eevee says. "This is Danny."

I extend my hand. "It's nice to meet you, Mr. Solomon."

He gives me a once-over, then shakes my hand. His grip is strong, like a warning. "Call me Sid."

"Did Mom call?"

He nods. "Danny, will you excuse us for a moment?"

Eevee follows him to the kitchen. I can hear their voices but can't make out what they're saying. The books on the shelves are all statistics, statistics and more statistics. There's one about the brain. And another book on statistics. Finally, they walk back into the room.

"Have a seat, Danny." He motions to the couch and sits again in the chair in the corner. Eevee sits across from me.

"Are you a friend from school?" he asks.

I clear my throat. "I met her at the—"

"English," she says. "Danny's in my English class."

"Then you're a sophomore as well?"

My brain is running on empty. Eevee gives a small nod and I stammer, "Y-yeah. Yes, sir. Sophomore."

He takes a hard look at me. "I'm sorry to hear you're having trouble at home." He continues to scrutinize. Deciding if I'm trouble or not.

I sweep the hair out of my eyes. Try not to look like a freak. "Thanks. It's . . . uh . . ."

"No need to divulge." He holds up a hand. "You're welcome to stay here. If you can follow the rule. Eve, will you please tell him the rule?"

She angles her body so he can't see her roll her eyes. Keeps her voice straight, though, and says, "My actions will not have a negative impact on myself or others in this home."

"Thank you." Sid leans back, crosses his arms. "Does that sound reasonable, Danny?"

Is this guy for real? "Yes, sir."

"Then we're agreed. You may stay in Eve's room."

"Oh," she says. "I thought he'd stay on . . ." She looks at the couch.

"Most people don't have the luxury of two bedrooms to call their own."

She nods.

"Will you show our guest the way?"

She stands, so I stand, too, and follow her past the kitchen to the hallway. She pushes open the first door on the right. "Bathroom." And the next door on the left. "My room." She holds it open for me. "I mean, *your* room."

I stop before going in and look at her. Same dark hair. Same eyes. Same girl, but so different. A gazillion thoughts tumble through my brain, everything I should say to her, but all I get out is "Thanks."

Her head tilts to the right and she smiles. "We can talk more tomorrow." Her voice sounds tired or sad. Can't tell which.

"Sounds good." I walk into her room.

She starts to leave, but turns back. "Don't touch anything, okay?" I nod. And with that, she's gone.

Don't touch anything? There isn't much in here to touch. The place hardly looks lived in. The bed takes up most of the space. Gray comforter and pillows. Black dresser in the corner. Matching nightstand and silver lamp. A poster of Einstein, which seems unusual for a teenage girl, but whatever. The closet is pretty much empty inside. A couple of shirts on hangers. Jeans folded on a shelf. There's nothing really *her* about the room.

I peel off the jacket and toss it on the bed. Kick off the shoes and my feet feel ten pounds lighter. I stretch. Sit on the edge of the mattress and rub my banged-up knee.

What now? If I were home, I'd play some Carnage or hang out with Germ.

Germ. Where was he when all that happened? Did he get hurt, or worse, caught? Is he lost somewhere in this crazy place like me?

I jump to my feet, keyed up all of a sudden, and pace around the room. Feels like the walls are closing in. What if Germ needs help and I'm stuck here? Wherever here is. I can't just sit around. I need answers.

The nightstand beside the bed has a single drawer. I pull it open. Inside, there's a journal and a pencil.

Einstein's eyes are on my back. *Don't touch anything.*

The cover has that drawing of a naked guy in a circle with his arms stretched out. What do they call him? Venturian Man? The art makes me think of Eevee. Her red dress and killer heels. Hair up off her shoulders. The way she smiled. The way her body felt against mine.

It's like she doesn't remember.

Just as my fingers touch the journal, there's a knock at the door. The pencil rattles as I slam the drawer shut and I'm off the bed, standing at attention.

"Danny?" Mr. Solomon—Sid—calls through the door. "Would you like something to eat?"

I shake out my hands. Clear my throat. "Yeah. That'd be great."

Sid and I sit at the kitchen table, eating pita chips with hummus and working on a crossword.

"Five-letter word for 'meticulous.'"

I shove a loaded chip in my mouth and make a thinking face. "Meticulous . . . meticulous . . ." Maybe three brain cells are working on the clues. The rest are working out how I got here. Either way, I'm coming up with zilch.

"Fussy." Sid pencils in the boxes. "F-U-S-S-Y." Takes a swig of his kale juice. He's an oddball. Nice. But weird.

"So you have Ms. Fischbach, too?" he asks.

"What?"

"For English. Eve is always complaining about that class."

I fake it. "Yeah. It's pretty awful."

"Well, I'm glad to know she has a friend in there." He doesn't sound glad. "Are you good at English?" He looks at me over his glasses.

"Pretty good." I don't have to lie this time.

"Maybe you can help her. English isn't her strongest subject. I assist as I can, but we usually end up arguing. She can be . . ." He points to the crossword. "Fussy."

I think of her hand slinking up the back of my neck. She didn't even know my name. Not my idea of fussy. "When did she start painting?"

"Painting?" He shakes his head. "Eve doesn't have time for frivolous distractions."

"But she's apprenticed to that famous guy. Bosca?" I load hummus onto a chip and pop it in my mouth.

"You must be mistaken," Sid says slowly, like I don't speak the same language. "Eve's focus is academics. She's on target for Ivy League. Perhaps even overseas study. I'd be thrilled either way, of course."

"Well, the Education Panels will make that call, won't they?"

"Is that how they do things in the remedial track?"

My laugh catches in my throat and I choke. He thinks I'm an idiot. When I finally stop coughing, I open my mouth to argue, but decide to switch subjects instead. "Do you have a city map I can borrow?"

Surprised, he sets down the crossword. "Yes. Just a moment."

He disappears to another room while I slam a few more hummus chips, a plan forming in my mind.

"Here you go," he says when he returns. He hands me a folded map with PHOENIX in blazing red letters across the front.

"Thanks. I'll only need it for an hour or so."

"Take your time." He returns his attention to the crossword.

I push away from the table. "If you don't mind, I think I'll call it a night. Thanks again for letting me crash here."

"You're welcome. If you need anything else, let me know."

I tap the map against my palm as I walk down the hall to Eevee's room. Once inside, I unfold it and spread it across the bed, fish through my pockets for a scrap piece of paper and grab the pencil from the drawer.

First task: find my house. Second task: find Germ.

My eyes scan the map, searching out anything familiar in the minuscule street names. Takes me forever to find Eevee's street. This feels impossible. I roll onto my back, overwhelmed.

"What am I going to do?"

Einstein stares down at me. He doesn't have a clue either.

7

EEVEE

Saturday morning, the sun hazes through the bedroom window, pulling me from sleep. I turn over and cover my eyes, but a thought bubbles up through the fog in my brain. Something I need to remember. It nags at me, bobbing at the edge of my—

The knock at my door startles it away. I crawl out of bed and shuffle to the door where Mom, still in her nightgown, holds out the phone. "Your father."

And then I remember: there's a strange boy sleeping next door.

It's Saturday. I'm geocaching with Warren at ten. Better warn him about Danny. "What time is it?"

Mom shakes her head and pushes the phone into my hands. I wait for her to leave. "Hello?"

"I found a note on the table this morning." Dad sounds happy, like he does when he's completed a challenging statistical diagram. "It says *Off to find answers. Thanks for everything. Danny.*"

"You mean he's gone?"

"Looks like it."

"He didn't say where he was going?"

"Last night he asked to borrow a map, but he left it here beside the note."

Where did he go? To the foster home? I don't know what to think. Should I be worried?

"It's better this way," Dad says. "You don't need the distraction. Not with midterms coming up."

"Midterms," I mumble, my mind spinning.

"See you Sunday for dinner?"

"Dinner. Sunday."

And like that, everything goes back to normal.

I meet Warren at our usual spot: the lava rock in his front yard. He stands on top of his tiny mountain, watching the sky through a pair of binoculars.

"See anything good up there?"

"Ducks. A 747." He looks at me, jumps back like he's seen something horrific and stumbles off the rock. "Oh." He clutches his chest. "It's just you, Solomon."

"Hilarious. Are you ready to go or what?"

"Affirmative. How was the ballet?"

I follow him inside his house, relieved I don't have to tell him about Danny. Those two have a volatile past, to put it mildly. "Last night was bizarro."

"It's ballet. What did you expect?" He pushes open the door. "Mom! Departure imminent!"

Mrs. Fletcher drives us to the mall, where we suck down milk shakes, search for geocaches tucked away in storefronts and planters, avoid security guards and debate the finer points of superheroes.

"Superman versus Wolverine."

"Easy." Warren steps one foot in front of the other along a line of tile, as if he's walking a tightrope. "Wolverine has healing factor. Batman versus Daleks."

"Batman could just run them over with the Batmobile."

"Nah. They'd zap him before he got close enough. Plus, they can fly."

"Send a memo to Alfred. Tell him to get to work on an anti-extermination gadget."

Warren takes off through the mall doing his best Dalek impersonation. "Exterminate! Exterminate!" Soccer moms and store clerks gape at the begoggled nerd boy, but Warren is unfazed.

We find our final geocache (a magnetic minicache stuck in a pipe valve) by Java's Last Stand. We take turns adding our names to the log and using Warren's smartphone to track our find on the geocaching website. Warren holds out the phone for me to see. "Three o'clock. Time to go to Mac's."

Marcus McAllister is the most brilliant teacher at Palo Brea, if not the world. We had him last year for biology; this year we're in his honors chemistry class, as well as his advanced study in theoretical physics. Only a few students test into the program, and Warren and I took top placement. It means we take multiple science classes each semester, but it's so worth it. Mac has become more than a teacher to us. He's a mentor. I'd even go so far as to call him a friend. My parents love this, of course. Someone with major credentials will write my college recommendation letters. What could be better?

Warren and I spend as much time as we can at Mac's shop, helping him with projects and listening to his stories about when he worked with Boeing and NASA. Rumor has it he's associated with a lot of alphabet agencies, but whenever Warren and I start asking too many questions, he just smiles or shrugs. His greatest accomplishment, he says, is having kept his Van Halen *1984* concert shirt in mint condition.

We find Mac lying on the floor of the shop, the hangar-like structure he built next to his house, where he does his fabrication work. His mask is pulled down over his face and he's welding the base of an enormous cage that reaches halfway to the ceiling. The Beatles echo through the air. *Lucy in the sky with diamonds.*

"What is that, a pet carrier for mountain lions?" I ask.

He lifts the welding mask. "Close. Support frame for an entertainment center. It's for a custom home up in Cave Creek."

You'd think a brilliant guy like Mac wouldn't have to supplement his income building staircases and entertainment centers and stuff, but apparently teaching doesn't pay very well.

He slides out from under the structure and hobbles a bit when he stands. "You guys ready to work? Get your gear."

We walk together over to the supply shelves at the far side of the shop. As I reach for a pair of gloves, something catches my eye. The door to the shop's back room—usually closed—stands open, offering a glimpse of some huge piece of equipment draped in blue tarps. I elbow Warren and nod toward whatever it is.

We inch over for a closer look, but Mac's voice from behind stops us. "Given any more thought to the science fair?" He closes the door.

"We're still debating." I pull on the gloves as we follow him back to the other side of the shop. Mac hands me a length of angle iron, and I clamp it in place according to the blueprint spread out on the floor. If I completely fail at science, at least I can get a job welding. Dad would be thrilled.

"What's to debate?" Mac places the nozzle of the welder to the edge of the iron, squeezes the trigger and stitches a perfect seam. Flipping up the helmet, he blows on the lingering glow. "You come up with an idea, do the work, win the fair. No big deal. This is your year." He flips down the mask again and his voice sounds hollow. "Trust me."

I wait for him to finish the next weld, the liquid metal sizzling like bacon. "Warren wants to study bugs."

He stops the torch. "Bugs?"

"No I don't!" Warren makes a face. "I said asteroids."

We bicker as we work. Mac suggests different projects, but none of them stick. Nothing feels right. I don't understand why we're having such a hard time agreeing on a topic. Last year was so easy. Practical applications of carbonite cryonics. We would have won, too, if it hadn't been for Centennial High's team and their solar kit for standard combustion engines. Classic pandering to the eco crowd.

Soon the conversation turns from the science fair to the Large Hadron Collider, which naturally leads to black holes and time travel. One way or another, we always eventually end up talking about black holes and time travel.

"If only we had a time machine," Warren says. "Then we could travel to *after* the science fair and find out what our entry was."

"Except you can't—"

"I know, I know." Warren waves off Mac's correction. "You can't travel to the future because it hasn't happened yet. But what if you could?"

He launches into an excited monologue on all the things he'd do if he could travel into the future, most of which are unethical, not to mention the chaos he'd create, spawning paradox after paradox.

A lightning flash of a thought strikes me: what if the Danny on my doorstep is from the far-distant future? Mac and Warren's banter fades to white noise as the train of logic chugs through my brain, gathering steam.

It could explain why he was so disoriented. Why nothing here was familiar to him. Why he expected to see things *un-familiar* to me, like Spectrum—whatever that is—and heightened security. But if Danny is from the future . . .

Logic derails and crashes to a halt.

"Why does he look like himself?"

Warren asks, "What?" as Mac asks, "Who?" and I realize I've said it out loud.

"Uh, nothing." I give a little laugh.

Warren makes a *weirdo* face and they go back to their what-ifs. Mac checks the blueprints and points to a length of flatiron.

"We should build a time machine for the science fair," Warren announces, sliding the metal from the supply pile and handing it to me.

"That would be awesome, if it were possible." I pass it to Mac, who smirks, flips his welding mask down and tackles the next weld.

8

Danny

Sunday, just before the sun goes down, I knock on her dad's door. I tried her mom's first, but there was no answer.

After a moment, the handle turns and the door opens. Sid looks surprised, then disappointed to see me. "Eve," he says, "you have a visitor."

There's the sound of footsteps before she scoots around to stand in front of him. "You."

Unlike her dad, she looks happy. Looks amazing, actually. It's all I can do not to hug her, I'm so relieved to see a familiar face.

"Well, let him in." Her mom nudges Eevee to the side. "Hello again . . ."

"Danny," Eevee and I both say at the same time.

"That's right." She smiles. She has really big teeth. "Danny. We were just having dinner. Would you like to join us?" She tries to smooth Eevee's hair but Eevee shoos her away.

"We'll be back in a second," Eevee says, and shuts the door behind her. Standing closer to me, she cringes.

I must stink worse than I thought. "Sorry."

"Where did you go?"

Where *didn't* I go? My feet throb from pounding concrete. Every step, I told myself I was getting closer to home, but every step I was wrong. From my jeans pocket, I pull out the paper with the scrawled-on directions and the creases worn from folding and unfolding. There's a hole in the center where the paper finally gave way. "I made a plan." I hand it to her. "To find my parents and Germ. To figure out what's going on. But the things that were supposed to be there weren't. I got lost, and my parents . . ."

She holds up the paper and reads. "You walked all that way? That must have taken you . . ."

"About a day and a half."

"Right." She hands the paper back to me. I refold it and shove it back into my pocket, ignoring the printout from the library that's also in there. "Where did you stay last night?" she asks.

"A park somewhere down on . . . Dunlap? Northern? Can't remember."

Her mouth hangs open. "Why didn't you call me? Or come back here?"

"I didn't have your number. And didn't think I'd need it." I swipe the hair from my eyes. "I just kept walking, and then it was dark and I saw the park and thought I'd just stop and rest, but when I woke up, it was morning."

She shakes her head. "If you'd just stayed here we could have worked on this together. Whatever. It doesn't matter now. Do you want to come in? Have some dinner?"

"That would be great, but I . . ." I make a face.

"Yeah. You do smell pretty bad. Okay, listen." She puts her hand on the doorknob. "Just go along with whatever I say."

Inside, her parents sit at the dining table. Clearly, we've interrupted their conversation. Sid looks annoyed, but Judy smiles. "Come in," she says. "Sit down."

"Is it okay if he gets cleaned up first?" Eevee asks.

"Oh." Judy looks me over, like she's just noticed I'm covered in ick. "Sid?"

He stands up from the table. "Of course. Follow me. You remember where the bathroom is?"

"I'll keep your dinner warm until you're ready," Judy says. She goes to the kitchen and I follow a grumpy Sid down the hall.

●

Best. Shower. Ever.

I crank the tap as hot as I can stand. Gotta burn this funk off of me. The water rains over my head and down my chest. I scrub until it stings and then let the water scorch the grunge away. Wish I could wash the confusion away, too.

After, I squeeze as much water as I can from the tangle of hair I've somehow acquired and wipe the fog off the mirror. This body is a wreck. A map of angry scars. The front is bad. The back makes the front look like a skin-care ad. I lean in close and stare into eyes that aren't truly mine. I'm in there. When I pull the hair back and smile, I almost look like me.

Sid left clean clothes on the counter. Sweatpants and a Yale shirt. I pull them on, drag the towel over my hair again and wipe everything down. I already feel guilty accepting their charity; last thing I want is to leave them with a mess.

I hear their voices in the other room.

Sid: Why do you even know this boy?

Judy: Give her some space.

Sid: I just don't like any of this.

They stop talking when I walk into the room. The food smells so good I could die. "Thanks for the shower. For everything." I stand there awkwardly, wondering if I'm really welcome. Wondering if I should stay or go.

"Your dinner's here." Judy pulls a chair out.

"Thanks," I say, "but I don't want to cause any problems."

Eevee's face pleads. Sid's looks conflicted. His knuckles are white around his fork and knife, but his voice stays calm. "Join us. Please."

"Thank you." I take a seat.

The conversation's as normal as it can be. The only challenge is following along without shoveling all the food into my face at once. They talk about their jobs and about weather and some welding project Eevee's doing. I didn't know she could weld, but I'm not surprised.

Sid leans his elbows on the table. "Pardon my asking, Danny, but you're not going to up and disappear again, are you?"

"*Sid,*" Judy hisses.

"It's a valid question. If he's staying at my house, he needs to understand my door isn't a turnstile." Sid looks at me, expecting my answer.

"No, sir."

"Good." He takes a bite of pot roast.

Eevee jumps into the conversation. "Does this mean he can stay here?"

He chews, swallows. "A little while longer." He wipes his mouth with his napkin. "Under one condition. You help Eevee with her English homework."

"Dad." Her neck flushes and the pink spreads to her face.

He levels his eyes at me. "What do you say?"

That's it? Easy. "Sure," I answer. "I can do that."

"Excellent." He sets his napkin on the table and stands. "I could use a drink. Anyone need anything while I'm up?"

"Dessert." Judy collects the dishes.

When they're out of the room, Eevee mutters, "Well, that was awkward." She lowers her voice. "I can't believe you slept in the park. Weren't you scared?"

"A little." I think of the shadowed hollow where the evergreens grew together and their branches reached almost to the ground. The bark scratched at my back, but I felt pretty safe. Safer than I expected, actually. There's no one watching here. "In a way, I felt kind of free."

"But what if something had happened to you?"

I lean toward her and whisper. "Eevee, something *has* happened to me."

She leans in, too. "Right, but I mean, like, if someone hurt you."

I look at her dark, round eyes. The way her throat moves when she swallows. My mind races back to that night at the museum. The taste of her lips, her neck. "How did I end up sitting next to you in that class?" She seems startled, but doesn't move when I take her hand and run my thumb along her fingers. "I mean, of all places, and after what happened that night we met?"

She searches my face.

"You really don't remember, do you?" I can see the answer in her eyes. "I might not be the best kisser in the world, but I didn't think I was so bad you'd actually *forget*."

She snatches her hand back. "Kiss? You?"

"That awful, huh?"

"No, it's just . . ." She shifts in her seat, folds her hands in her lap. "I wouldn't . . ."

I sit back in my chair and cross my ankle over my knee. Try to cover the hurt by playing it cool. "Well, whatever. Thanks for helping me out. This sure beats dumpster dining."

"What? You didn't . . ."

"Where did you think I picked up that stench?"

"Here we are." Judy walks into the room balancing plates of chocolate cake. Sid follows with a bottle of sparkling water. We eat and chat and everyone is friendly and uses their best manners, but the whole time, I'm baffled. How could she not remember?

9

EEVEE

Monday morning my eyes snap open. I have to warn Warren about Danny. I log on to chat but he's offline. Maybe he's sick and won't be going to school. Then I notice the time. A quick peek out the window confirms my fear. He's already waiting for me on the lava rock. The sunlight glints off his goggles.

I dress in a panic and head out to face the inevitable.

"They're up there, Solomon," he says, staring into the sky. "Right now. Hundreds of meteors, streaking through the atmosphere." He zooms his hands at me, making explosive motions in my face. Then he looks over my shoulder and his expression morphs to disgust. "Why is Danny Ogden walking out of your dad's house?"

After dinner last night, I'd told Danny to meet me out here this morning. My plan was to wake up early to talk to Warren first. That plan failed. "He needed a place to stay." I cringe.

"And he chose your dad's house because . . . ?"

"He's in trouble and came to me for help?"

Warren crosses his arms. Stony-faced king of the lava rock.

I watch Danny walking toward us. He's wearing a pair of Dad's khakis and a polo. His hair hangs down in long, ragged strands. Rocker boy meets junior engineer. He looks ridiculous. Under different circumstances, I would have laughed, but not with Warren smoldering behind me. I turn back to face him. "It's complicated."

"Apparently."

"I can explain—" Unfortunately, Danny's arrival cuts me off before I have the chance.

"Hi." He pushes the hair out of his eyes and sticks out his hand. "I'm Danny."

Warren hops down from the rock. "I'm outta here."

This is not how it was supposed to go. "Wait."

But there's no stopping Warren once his mind is made up. He walks away, his backpack bouncing with each step. I don't know what to do but I'm sure anything I try right now will be wrong.

"What's his problem?" Danny's at my side.

"He doesn't like you."

"I can see that. Why?"

"Because you've tormented him since sixth grade."

"But I've never seen him before."

"What?" I turn to face him, my arms crossed. "You stuffed him in a locker."

He blinks and looks shocked and stifles a laugh. "I did not."

"You most certainly did. And don't even think of laughing. You just about ruined him."

His face drops to serious and he swallows. "What happened?"

Is he faking? How does he not know this? I consider sparing him the details, but decide brutal honesty is best.

"One day in sixth grade PE, you and your friends attacked Warren in the boys' locker room. You stripped off all of his clothes and crammed him in a locker, then took off laughing. You left him there alone, in the dark. Hours later, some kids who were there for after-school soccer practice heard him screaming. The janitor had to cut the lock to get him out. He went into hiding for weeks. You were suspended, of course."

The memories of those days come flooding back. I think of how Warren wouldn't talk to anyone. How the day he finally returned to school he was wearing aviator goggles and how he's worn some version ever since. How he wouldn't raise his hand in class or sit with anyone at lunch or make eye contact, even with *me*. It wasn't until years later he confided about the nightmares and his newfound fear of the dark. "He was a completely different Warren after that."

"Wow." Danny's voice is thin. "I'm an asshole."

"Pretty much." I take a deep breath and let it out slowly. Emotions will only interfere with getting to the bottom of the problem. Namely, why Danny doesn't remember any of this.

"Okay. So, who are you really?" I ask.

"Danny Ogden."

"No. You're not."

"Then who am I? And what's happened to me?"

"No idea. But if anyone can figure this out, it's him." I point down the street.

Which means I have to find a way to get Warren to listen to me. Which means first I have to get him to talk to me again. I shoulder my messenger bag and start walking to school. "Come on. Maybe we can catch up to him."

Danny doesn't budge.

"What? You're not going to school?"

"I think I should try again to find my parents." The way he says it, it sounds like there's something he's not telling me.

A quick glance at my phone sends my heart racing. I am super, über late. "Fine." I grab a pen from my bag and scribble my number on his hand. "But if you get lost again, call me."

10

Danny

I watch Eevee walk down the street and, for the millionth time, think back to the night we first met.

For weeks they'd had us under curfew, their typical response to unspecified threats. No one was allowed out after dark—for our own protection, of course. Anyone caught breaking curfew faced fines, interrogation, the usual. As always, we adapted, changing our personal routines to comply. Then, just as quickly as they'd initiated the regulation, they lifted it. To an extent. We could move freely after sundown within a secured zone: namely, the lower downtown corridor, all conveniently arranged to coincide with the opening of a new exhibit at the Phoenix Art Museum. I was sure it would be mostly propaganda but I didn't care. I would have watched paint dry or cars idle just to *be out*. The fact that I didn't have a ticket didn't stop me either. I'd find a way in. Somehow.

After clearing facial recognition and pat-downs, I boarded the light rail with my approved group. By the time we reached

Lower Downtown, the sun was setting, turning the sky to sherbet soup. Our group moseyed along the rail lines, joining up with the other security-approveds slowly making their way to the museum. The show started at seven, but no one hurried. Instead, people carried on conversations, pointing out this and that. The spinning restaurant at the top of the Hyatt. The dancing statues in front of the Herberger Theater. A busker belted out patriotic songs at the corner of Central and McDowell. I listened for a bit, wondering if he'd slip any anti lyrics in, but he stuck to the script. Everyone did. From the lampposts and building cornices, Spectrum kept watch.

I shadowed a group of women, shuffling behind them toward the museum entrance, and slipped away to the side door when I thought there might be a break in cover.

The door was locked.

I leaned back against the building, trying to figure out my next move. I could either hang out there or risk my luck and slip outside the authorized zone. Hit Falcon Park, maybe. See if there were any other artists around.

An old man walked toward me. "Is this the entrance?"

"Around the front."

He thanked me and left. I tried the knob again, just to be sure. Still locked. Time to find another way in or move on.

I'd only taken a couple of steps when the door hinges creaked behind me. I turned and saw a girl in a red dress.

A gorgeous girl.

A little red dress.

She took off her shoes and used one to prop open the door. Then she leaned back against the wall, her eyes closed.

The streetlight spilled across her face and shoulders, leaving a shadow in the hollow of her neck.

I tucked my hands in my pockets and waited. Watched. When she finally opened her eyes and saw me, her mouth made the shape of a perfect O. Then she replaced that O with a smile that sent chills down my arms.

"You're not supposed to be here," she said.

I shrugged. A dare.

She looked left and right, moving only her eyes. Then she slunk toward me, stopping just inches away. She leaned in and touched her lips to mine. Snaked her hand around the back of my neck and pressed that red dress against me.

What was I supposed to do, being kissed like that by a girl who looked the way she did?

A. Maze. Ing.

A car over on Central honked and she stepped back, one hand still on my chest and her lipstick smudged outside the lines. The neckline of her dress moved with her breathing. She adjusted her shoulder strap, smiled and turned back toward the door.

"Hang on," I said.

She looked over her shoulder.

So many questions. I chose the least obvious. "Why?"

She shrugged, then picked up her shoes and walked back through the door, leaving me in the shadows.

Outside.

I tried to make sense of what had just happened, but came up empty.

After a moment, the hinges creaked again. The long arm that'd just been wrapped around me held it open.

Don't have to tell me twice.

But as soon as I walked in, she was gone. If it weren't for the lingering scent of her perfume—sharp, like ginger—I probably would have thought I'd imagined it all.

I searched for her through the back rooms and side galleries until I ended up in the main exhibit hall. The place was packed. Wall-to-wall people wandering around whispering, drinking wine. From what I remember, the art was incredible, but it was pretty much lost on me at that point. All I could think about was her. I scanned the crowds. Room after room, nothing.

When I was about to give up, I caught a glimpse of red disappearing behind a huge sculpture of two black spheres. I pushed my way through the crowd, pissing off lots of people in the process. Turned a corner and saw her leading a group of suits toward a painting. Couldn't hear what she said, but I was transfixed by the way she talked with her hands.

I grabbed some poor museum volunteer by the sleeve. "Who is that?"

He followed my pointing finger. "Eve Solomon."

"Is this her work?" He raised his eyebrow at the way I was gripping his sleeve. I let go. "Sorry."

He straightened his shirt. "She's *an* artist," he said, "but not *the* artist. Antonio Bosca is *the* artist. Miss Solomon is Mr. Bosca's apprentice."

"Eve Solomon," I whispered. The guy rolled his eyes and walked away. I watched her circulate through the room, pointing out the details of Bosca's artwork, laughing when her audience laughed and answering questions with her delicious, smudged lips. At one point, her eyes flicked over to me and

she paused midword. Then she finished what she'd been saying, still smiling.

Standing here in this upside-down version of Phoenix, I
can just see the back of Eevee's head as she turns the corner of
the street and disappears from view.

She's nothing like the dangerous girl who kissed me without warning. That girl fascinated me for obvious reasons.
This Eevee, though. She's like one of those van Eyck paintings
where the closer you look, the more you see. Or an Escher
drawing where, just when you think you've got it figured out,
the whole thing flips.

She's a puzzle.

And so is this Phoenix.

I pull the printout from my pocket. Better get moving. It's
time I start figuring out how I got here. And how to get back.

11

EEVEE

I dart into first-hour physics. Class has already started, and Mac is standing at the front of the room, lecturing from behind the demonstration table. A contraption of coiled metal and wire takes up most of his workspace. As he talks, he paces back and forth, tossing an apple into the air. I break up Warren and Missy's whisperfest when I take my seat between them. She looks annoyed that I interrupted their conversation. Warren turns his back to me.

"Hey."

He doesn't look up.

Mac continues to talk, his eyes distant, like he's talking out loud to himself rather than teaching a class. "The repulsive force on diamagnetic materials is too small to measure when using a standard electromagnet." He trades out the apple for a marker and writes a formula on the whiteboard. The class follows suit, copying the information down.

The zipper of my backpack is painfully loud. I pull out my

physics notebook and a sharp pencil, then zip the bag back up and set it on the floor. Ugh. If anyone missed the fact that I was late to class, it's obvious now.

Mac picks up the apple again. "But in the presence of a hybrid magnet, the magnetic field counterbalances gravity."

I scribble down the formula while trying to keep up with Mac's lecture and also trying to ignore the looks passing between Warren and Missy.

"Of course," Mac continues, "electrons don't like being in magnetic fields. How do they react?"

A number of hands go up. He chooses someone at the back of the room.

"They modify rotation to compensate?"

"Correct." Mac tosses the apple and catches it. "They work in opposition to the external influence."

Warren's arm slides a note across our table. My mood lifts. Maybe the situation isn't as bad as I thought.

I reach for the note, but he jerks it away and slides it past me.

To Missy

Missy smiles and takes the note with a dainty index finger and thumb. Warren pulls his arm back.

"If nature is anything, it's consistent," Mac says. "Whenever a force disturbs or acts against it, the reaction is always negative. Behold." He drops the apple into the cylinder and switches the electromagnet on. The apple rises inside the tube, bobbing slightly. The class whispers a collective "Whoa."

Except Missy. She unfolds the note. I'm torn between the

coolness of the experiment and my curiosity about what War-ren has written.

"As long as the external force is present, the internal force reacts. The result, at least in this case, is levitation."

I set my pen down and pretend to stretch, leaning back so I can peer over Missy's shoulder.

Tonight, the note says. *7 p.m. Rooftop.*

12

Danny

My first stop is the foster house, not so much for info, but for resources. I move fast, retracing the route the truck guy took on Friday until, after a long walk, I finally find the correct street. I know the house by the half-dead evergreen with its brown, thistly branches, the garbage can that lies tipped on its side, and the bits of trash littering the front yard.

I lift the latch on the gate and skulk around the back of the house, hoping no one's home. The window where "my" room is doesn't have a screen. I jimmy it until it slides open.

The place is disgusting. Junk all over the floor. Walls covered in strange flags and disturbing posters. A stop sign nailed to the ceiling over the door.

I can totally see the guy who lives in this room torturing that Warren kid.

The guy who lives in this room is tortured himself.

I listen for voices, but the house is still. Perfect. I find a duffel bag and ransack the place. Stuff some clothes in it. They're all rocker junk. Skinny jeans and flannels. In the back of the closet I find a pair of Vans and an old skateboard. Nice. I grab a watch and some other odds and ends. Under the mattress I find some trashy magazines and rolled-up bills. I leave the zines, stuff the money in my pocket, then stop to look around. I gotta be smart about this. Make it look like nothing's out of the ordinary. So I slide the window shut. Grab the board and walk through the house. Leave a note on the kitchen table.

> *Gone for a couple of days.*
> *—Danny*

I leave through the front door, knowing the easy part of today's plan is behind me.

The board *cla-clacks* down the sidewalk. The deck sags pretty bad, but at least the wheels aren't too soft. The directions are still in my pocket, but I have the route pretty much memorized. West on Greenway Road, north on 67th, east on Juniper.

After I get there comes the hard part.

For now, though, it's push off and ride, push off and ride. The rumble of the wheels keeps me grounded. I ease into a turn, pop an ollie, and biff. Get up, brush myself off. The guy who owns this body is totally not a skater. I have to fight just to keep steady. At least, when I'm moving, The Hair stays out of my face.

It made me nervous, walking into that library on Saturday.

I thought for sure the woman at the information desk was going to kick me out when I asked for help. But she just smiled over her glasses and walked me over to the computers.

"Anyone can use them?"

"Yes, of course."

"For free?"

She nodded. "If you need anything else, you know where to find me." She started to walk away, but I stopped her. I don't know if it was the look on my face or what it was I told her I was looking for, but she pulled up a chair beside me and helped me search.

I'm just glad I found out about my parents after she'd been called away to another task.

She'd directed me to the County Recorder's Office. I typed Dad's name into the search field, selected Death Certificate from the menu, and there it was. Official seal, signatures, everything.

Parker Ogden. Cause of death: blunt trauma as result of traffic accident. Place of disposition: Sonoran Valley Cemetery.

I did the same search for Mom.

Rebecca Ogden. Cause of death: blunt trauma as result of traffic accident. Place of disposition: Sonoran Valley Cemetery.

As I printed out the information, the pieces fell into place. Dead parents. Foster home. The date of death on the screen said it happened when I was eleven, so I guess that explains why I changed districts and enrolled in Eevee's school.

But.

Friday morning I said goodbye to Mom before heading over to Germ's. Before the last gig with Red December. Before the explosion.

Dad and I were going to take the boat out on Saturday. We heard they'd lifted restrictions on the marina, and it'd been a long time since we'd done anything fun like that.

My wheel catches a rock and the board stops dead, flinging me forward. I try to keep from falling, but my banged-up knee is useless. I kick the board across the sidewalk. It lands upside down. I kick it again and again, yelling for no reason. When it skids to a stop, I watch the wheels spin.

If I'm here, who's there? Who went boating with Dad?

And who is in the ground at Sonoran Valley Cemetery?

I set the board right side up again and take off, dodging the rocks, pushing myself faster, faster.

⬤

I've never been to a cemetery before. Don't know what I expected, but it's not this. The gravestones are flat on the ground, not standing upright like you see in movies. Most are decorated with faded silk flowers and pinwheels. The place is massive. There's no way I'm going to find them.

I read as many names as I can as I walk along the drive, my board in my hands. Schwartz. Hernandez. Blake. Mullins. An old guy in a straw hat drives up in a golf cart.

"Can I help you, son?" He squints, even with his eyes shaded.

"I'm looking for someone. Two people, actually. Ogden?"

He makes a thinking face, closing one eye and puckering his mouth. Then he motions with his head. "Come on."

I take the passenger seat and lay the board across my lap. The golf cart starts with a jolt. "Recent?" he asks, steering the cart and peering out over the lawns.

"2008."

We pull up to a building the size of a large toolshed. He steps inside and returns with a notebook. Flips through the pages, muttering my last name under his breath. "Parker and Rebecca?"

My stomach caves.

"Bit of a walk. I'll take you."

He climbs back into the golf cart and we wind around another turn, past a wall of names and a quote carved into the granite. O DEATH, WHERE IS THY STING?

"Family?"

"My friend's parents," I lie. He stops the cart under a huge tree, near a stone bench. "About twenty paces that way." He points. "Take your time."

"Thanks."

The cart's wheels crunch the gravel as he drives away. Then I'm standing there by myself and I can't move.

I look up into the sky. Clouds breeze by. Leaves wave in the sunlight. It's a perfect day. A perfect, horrible, awful, terrible day. Why won't the ground open up and swallow me now?

"You come all this way for nothing?" My voice sounds small, not brave. I force one leg to move. Then the other. The sun glints off a gazing ball, and wind chimes ring nearby. I read the names out loud as I go.

"Rollins. Perkins. Dominguez."

Then I see them and my legs turn to liquid. I crouch down to keep from falling to my knees.

Their grave is simple. No flowers or pinwheels. Just a single bronze plaque edged by green grass, their names side by side with an infinity symbol between. I stare at it a long, long time. Like I'm waiting for the *Twilight Zone* music to start, or Germ to step out from behind a tree and tell me this is some kind of joke.

But he doesn't. And it's not.

13

EEVEE

Danny's not around when I get home from school. And he's not around for dinner either, which annoys Dad. I keep checking my phone, thinking maybe he's lost and I missed his call.

But no.

I sit on the tree stump in the strip of yard between Mom's and Dad's. Bugs circle under the streetlight, growing bright and then dim as they move into and away from the bulb. Every now and again one flies too close and smashes into the plastic or the pole. From down here, it's just a tapping sound. Up there, though, it must be cataclysmic. Movement beyond the bugs catches my eye. I peer through the light to Warren's rooftop across the street, where a figure sits alone.

It's got to be after seven. Where is Missy?

Despite my better judgment, I decide to find out.

He doesn't hear me ascend the ladder, but when I make the awkward transition to the roof, he turns around.

"Oh," he says, "it's you." Disappointed.

He's wearing the special-task-forces night-vision goggles he got for his thirteenth birthday, and a leather fighter-pilot jacket, despite the fact that it's 80° out. Also, his hair is combed.

He must really like her.

I'm not supposed to know about the note, so I need to proceed with caution. On a wooden tray nestled between the telescopes are Oreos, strawberries, *Star Wars* special-edition mugs and a bottle of white grape juice. "That's quite a spread for a solo rooftop spectacle."

"Clearly I was expecting someone." He sounds miserable, and looks it, too, sitting with his back to me, his shoulders slumped and his feet dangling off the edge of the roof.

"Want to talk about it?"

"Not really."

I scrape the toe of my shoe along the sandpaper shingles. "Do you want me to leave?"

He shrugs, but as I turn to go back to the ladder, he says, "You can stay if you want."

Walking along the rooftop can be tricky, especially when it's congested with all of Warren's observation equipment. Warren can walk the roof with the agility of a mountain goat, but me, I'm not so goat-footed.

"What's the show tonight?" I find a spot near the tray, beside a duffel bag.

"Lyrids meteor shower. Here." He hands me a pair of night-vision goggles. "You don't want to have these on for the show, but they're kind of fun for now."

I slip them over my head and the world is bathed in sea green. The rooftops and trees snap into clear focus. A man takes out the garbage. Another guy scoots around on a skateboard. The dog next door barks to be let inside.

Warren rummages through the duffel bag and pulls out what looks like a gun. For a fraction of a second, I panic. I know Warren is mad at me, but he can't be *that* kind of mad.

"Check this out." His voice sounds a little brighter. "It's a vintage Skywatch 3000 Instant Star and Constellation Identifier. I traded up with one of my raiding friends. Still works perfectly."

"You mean it's not a laser weapon?"

"I wish. Here." He hands it to me. "Just point and shoot."

I hold the gun up at the sky and he presses a button on the back. The thing bleeps and a woman's voice says, "Alkaid. Constellation: Ursa Major. Visual magnitude: 1-point-86. Right ascension: 10 hours, 67 minutes, 46 seconds."

"Cool." I carefully hand it back to him.

"Can you believe he traded the pop-top Death Star for it? Amateurs."

His smile drops and he goes back to sad Warren. Silence settles between us until, finally, he clears his throat. "I invited Missy Bivins over."

I can't say I know, so I don't say anything.

"She backed out at the last minute."

"So she was going to make it?"

"Yes."

"Well, that's good, right?"

"Guess so."

We sit in our silence and our goggles and this awkward distance between us. He eats an Oreo, so I follow suit. Next, a strawberry, and I do, too. We sip grape juice. Look around.

Sigh. Listen to the sounds of the neighborhood and wait for the meteors. It's like tiptoeing through land mines in foreign territory. I have no idea where to step next. When I can't stand it any longer, I clear my throat. "We need to talk about . . . stuff."

He doesn't say anything. Maybe he didn't understand what I meant. "About the thing with Danny."

"Do we have to do it now?"

"You'd rather just pretend it's not happening?"

"What *is* happening, Eevee?"

"Not what you think."

"Stoner-face bully staying at your dad's house isn't what I think?" He picks up an Oreo and chucks it over the side of the house. I watch it with the night vision until it falls out of sight.

"No. It's not what you think. And you just wasted a perfectly good Oreo."

He stands and paces the six feet of roof not occupied by astronomy equipment or food.

"Will you sit down and hear me out, please?"

He crosses his arms. He's stubborn like a goat, too.

"Fine. Don't sit. Just listen. Either Danny is having a mental breakdown, or he's from somewhere else."

"What does that mean?"

"Friday in English he woke up and ran out of class. I didn't think much about it. But then he showed up at my house that night saying he needed my help."

"Why you? Why not one of his loser friends?"

I choose my words with care. "He said I was the only person he knew."

"You? He doesn't know you. Not really."

"Right. Then he asked why there aren't security check-points and stuff here."

"What?"

"Wherever he's from, it's way different than here. He was really freaked out." I look at my hands. "He said he'd met me at a museum . . . and that I'd kissed him."

"Him?!" Now his wheels are turning. He sits down, facing me.

"I *know*. He's not who we think he is."

He considers this a moment, then shakes his head. "Nah. He's still Danny Ogden, resident cretin."

I shift my weight. The shingles get uncomfortable after a while. "You have to believe me, Warren. It's only been a couple of days, but he's definitely not the same guy who . . ." I don't have to finish the sentence.

He looks away. "Where's he from, then?"

"Well, my first thought was he's from the future."

He scoffs. "That's a pretty big leap."

"I know. That theory doesn't work, but he still isn't who we think he is."

"What did you tell your parents? Why is your dad letting him stay there?"

"That's another weird thing." I pick up a strawberry and take a bite. "The Danny we know lives with a foster family, but this Danny says he lives with his parents. Only he can't find them. Anyway, my parents took pity on him and let him stay."

"Pity on *him*? Why would anyone take pity on him?"

I think about how scared Danny looked when he showed

up at my door. "If I found myself lost and afraid, I'd want someone to help me."

"I can't see him fitting in at your dad's."

I shrug. "So far so good."

"So far? How long is he going to stay?"

"Until we figure out what happened to him."

"We? If you think I'm getting involved in this, think again, Solomon. This is your trip into Loserville, not mine."

He turns away, but I know how to win this game. "Suit yourself." I keep my voice cool. "But when it turns out to really be time travel or body snatchers or *whatever* awesome thing, I'll be the one getting the credit."

"You're totally out of your league."

"And you're totally in for a surprise." I eat an Oreo and watch him simmer.

"What if he's just having a bad drug trip?"

"I don't think so. My gut tells me he's clean."

He snorts. "Your gut. The compass of all scientific reason."

"Excuse me? Whose idea for cricket cryogenics won us a trip to the National Science Foundation youth conference? My gut's done us a lot of good."

He rolls his eyes. "So what am *I* supposed to do to help *your* stoner freak?"

"Talk to him. See if there's anything that sparks ideas or connections with that big brain of yours."

Want to win with Warren? Compliment his intelligence.

He lets out a dramatic sigh. "Okay, fine. But if he thinks he's going to push me around again . . ."

"He won't."

"Better not." He picks up the star gun and points it at the sky. The woman croons out the coordinates and particulars of the constellation Gemini, then silence settles again between us, only it's not the awkward kind this time.

"Warren," I say after a while. "I'm sorry your evening didn't go as planned, but thanks for talking to me about all this. No one gets me like you do." I hold out my fist. "Grok?"

"Grok." He bumps my fist with his own, then takes off his goggles. "About time to start."

It's been a while since I've seen his whole face. I pull my goggles off, too, and our shapes blur as my eyes adjust again to the dark.

We sit in silence, waiting for the light show. Two strangers in a strange new land.

Fifteen meteors later, I walk back across the street. The guy on the skateboard I'd seen from Warren's roof rolls toward me.

It's Danny.

"Wow, what happened to you?" I point at his long shorts and retro robot shirt. "You almost look normal."

"I almost feel normal." He stops the board with one foot on the ground. "Though I keep expecting patrols to come bust me for being out past curfew."

"We don't have curfew around here. Well, my dad does, but that's different. So, where did you get all this?"

"Raided the foster house," he says, skating away. "And went shopping."

"What about your parents?"

He flips the board and lands, skates a half circle around me and flips the board again. Either he didn't hear the question or he doesn't want to answer. "I talked to Warren," I say, louder.

He skates toward me and stops. "Great. What did he say?"

"Sounds like he's going to help. We're meeting him tomorrow after school."

From a standstill, he jumps up, flips the board over and lands on both feet. "God, it feels good to be out here."

"You *are* going to school tomorrow, right?"

He makes a face. "I don't see the point."

"You have to."

"Why?"

"Because it's what you're supposed to do."

"It's not my school."

True, but if my dad finds out he's ditching, he'll blow a gasket. "You should do the right thing for Danny. He isn't the best student."

"I figured that much."

"I'm serious."

"Eevee, I don't even know his schedule."

"Oh." I hadn't thought of that. "We'll get it from the office. No big deal."

He changes the subject. "Want a ride home?"

"No way." I step back. "That thing will cause me serious bodily harm."

"Come on." He sets the board back down and holds out his hand. "I won't let you fall."

I don't know Danny Ogden. I know *this* Danny Ogden even less. His eyes are kind, but can I trust him?

Guess we'll find out.

The wheels move when I step on. I grab his hand and try not to squeal.

What am I doing? If Warren sees this, he'll freak. Oh God, what if Dad is watching? Or worse, Mom? His hand is really soft. . . . Eevee Solomon, you've lost your mind. And your balance.

The board does a crazy swerve and I gasp.

"Bend your knees. It'll help."

I bend my knees. It does help. Until he grabs my other hand, and starts walking backward, taking the board and me with him.

"You're goofy."

"Goofy?!" I laugh. "*You're* goofy."

"No, I'm regular." He tries to let go of one of my hands but I grab it back. "Goofy means you're right-footed. Right foot in front."

"Oh. Of course." I'm an idiot. I shouldn't be on this thing. We're headed for the curb. I'm going to break my neck.

"Lean all your weight toward me, on your toes. . . . That's right."

He guides me into a turn away from the sidewalk, through the circle of streetlight. "See? It's not so bad." We stop in front of Mom's house and he helps me step off the board. "You just need some practice." The light throws shadows across his face. His hands are warm around mine.

"Thanks for the ride." My voice is quiet. "That was fun."

"You're welcome."

We're still holding hands.

"I should probably . . ." I glance over my shoulder at Mom's house.

"Right," he says. "I should, too."

"Good night."

He lets go first and my hands feel empty and bare. I tuck them into my pockets, smile and walk through the grass to the front door.

"Eevee!"

I turn back.

"What time tomorrow morning?"

"Seven-thirty."

He gives me a thumbs-up and skates toward Dad's. I watch him do one last flip and close the door behind me.

14

Danny

Why did I let her talk me into this?

The teacher looks like he's got something stuck up his butt. He paces back and forth in front of the whiteboard, pulling the cap off his dry-erase marker and forcing it back on. "Do you know the answer? No? Come on, guys. This one should be a no-brainer."

When I can't stand it anymore, I clear my throat and half raise my hand. He points the marker at me.

"Forty-two?"

He's so happy you'd think I just gave him a birthday present. "Yes! Excellent." He writes the numbers four and two really big under the problem and stands back to admire it like it's a Rembrandt or something.

Most of the class is comatose. The rest are goofing off.

I'm in loser hell.

Eevee took me to the office first thing this morning. Got me a copy of Danny's schedule. My schedule. This is our agreement: until we figure out how to get me back home, I lay low and do what I can to make things better for him—the other Danny. Which means going to class and being a good boy. I tried to explain to her that laying low for Danny would mean ditching school, smoking and probably knocking off a bank or something, but in the end she won. She can be really persuasive.

I look at the schedule. Next is PE. Can't wait.

"You have the rest of class to work on these problems," the teacher says. "I don't mind if you use your books, but no talking or sharing work." He starts passing out papers. Wakes up the droolers and tells a girl to put away her tunes. He lays a paper on my desk. He smells like bad cheese. I pull the pencil from my back pocket and look over the sheet.

Then, *zoom*. I rocket through the problems. Easy peasy. I write my name at the top and walk the paper up to the teacher's desk. He looks up. "You have a question?"

"No." I hand him the paper. "I'm done."

He raises an eyebrow. Takes the paper and looks it over. Raises both eyebrows. "I don't allow cheating in my class."

Dude.

"I didn't cheat." A couple of the losers look up, probably hoping there'll be a fight.

He reaches into his desk, pulls out another paper. Hands it to me with challenge written all over his face. "Prove it."

This is lame. I start to walk back to my chair.

"No, no," he says. "Right here." He points to an empty spot on his desk.

I saunter back, tapping the pencil against my leg. Then I

lean over the desk and rock the worksheet. Wham. Bam. Finish the last one with a flourish. Make my own Rembrandt and step back to admire it.

I got your challenge right here, cheese man.

He takes the paper from me and looks it over. Looks at me like I've just figured out world peace. "But . . ."

And it hits me how sad this is. The other Danny must be such a wasteoid. I turn off the attitude and turn on the good boy. "Just thought I'd start giving a damn. Darn. Sorry."

A smile takes over his face and he's back to birthday happy. I've obviously made his day. And that's cool, I guess. "This is great, Danny. Really great. You can take it easy the rest of class."

"Thanks."

A couple of the losers glare at me as I walk to my desk. As if my doing a little math threatens their existence somehow.

Pathetic.

●

All of the sidewalks at Palo Brea have these huge support beams shaped like S's that curve from the ground up to the awnings. They're a foot around, at least, and perfect for skating. Every time I pass one, my head fills with trick ideas. Wallie. Pop shove-it. Maybe if I hit it right I could even do a vertical grind.

I pass the spot where I'll meet Eevee later and look for her face in the crowd. There's probably a special place where all the smart kids go. Keep them separated from the imbecile masses.

"Ogden!"

I jerk my head toward the sound. See a group of guys by a garbage can outside a locker bay. They've got bad news written all over them.

I make the cool-guy chin nod and keep going, but they call again. "Og!" When I get closer, one says, "Hey, man, haven't seen you around."

These guys are hairy and rude and they stink. I wouldn't be surprised if they started picking mites off each other and eating them.

"Where you been?" This one's got to be the leader. He's not as hairy and his arm is slung over a girl's shoulders. She's wearing too much makeup. Trying too hard.

"Just been, you know, around."

One of the bigger monkeys laughs and imitates me like a doofus. "Just been around." That's right. Laugh it up, dumbass.

"You look like hell," the leader says.

Nice.

The girl pipes up. "I think you look good."

Nice.

Alpha monkey doesn't say anything, but he tightens his grip on her shoulder and she squirms. She knows the game she's playing. I'm tempted to tell her she's not my type, but it's probably best to keep my hole shut.

"I gotta run. Catch ya later." I start walking away, but the leader calls after me.

"You gonna be at Dean's Friday?"

I grimace. "Nah, man. Can't. Other plans."

"It's okay," he says. "You can bring her."

"Who?"

"That girl you were with this morning. Bring her. It's cool."

"Oh." I walk backward away from them. Like I'd ever in-vite Eevee to a party with these guys. Like she'd ever say yes. But I play along. For Danny's sake. "Um, yeah, I'll have to see about that."

I turn around and smack right into one of the S-beams. *Clong.* The sound rings through my brain and I stumble around, dazed. My buddies back there fall all over themselves laughing.

Nice.

I try to use the beam incident as an excuse to get out of PE but the coach says not unless I want to go see Nurse Clara. I don't. She might call the foster parents, and then who knows what would happen.

So I go with the flow. Try to deflect attention. Until I real-ize I have no clue how to get into my—Danny's—gym locker.

"Uh, Coach?" I interrupt him talking to a guy in a tie. Must be a teacher or someone. They both look at me like I'm being rude, which I guess I kind of am.

"I can't remember my locker combination."

The guy in the tie raises an eyebrow. Coach says, "This is getting old, Danny."

"Sorry."

"Look at me." Tie guy gets right in my face and says under his breath, "You high again?"

"No."

His eyes dart back and forth across mine.

"I'm not. I swear. Just can't remember the numbers."

He sneers and steps back. "I'll catch up with you later, Terry."

"Sounds good, Tom."

Tie guy leaves the locker room. "This way," Coach says, and I follow him to his office. He opens the bottom drawer of a filing cabinet and tosses clothes at me. "Go get changed."

He walks out of the office and announces, "Out to the track, guys. We're doing laps today."

Everyone groans and I'm still standing there holding a pair of green shorts and a school T-shirt. They both stink like, well, I don't even want to know.

This totally sucks. I blame Eevee.

The track runs around the football field. When I finally get out there, I try to catch up to the rest of the class. My knee is purple from the first day when I crashed it into the street. I push through the pain and pound my feet on the clay.

"How many left?" I ask the guy running closest to me, my words broken up with panting.

"How many what?" He's not having any problem running and talking.

"Laps," I wheeze. "How many laps?"

"I dunno. Ten?"

There's no way. This body has the lungs of an eighty-year-old smoker. I'm gonna die. My feet scuff along as I push myself to stay with the pack. Somehow, despite the coughing and wheezing, I manage to keep up. At the end of the run, I collapse on the grass of the football field. Coach stands over me, blocking out the sun.

"Good effort, Ogden," he says. "Nice to see you trying."

15

EEVEE

I press Warren's doorbell and hear it chime inside. "Come on, it couldn't have been that bad."

Danny crosses his arms. "Let's see. Today I was accused of cheating and of being stoned. I found out I'm friends with a pack of Neanderthals. I ran into one of those stupid sidewalk poles and made an ass of myself in front of everyone. Oh, and did I mention I have the lungs of an old smoker?"

I can't help but laugh. "Did anything good happen today?"

"No."

"Well, maybe our talk with Warren will change that."

The door opens. Warren is wearing his tinted goggles, the ones that hide his eyes. He doesn't say anything as he stands aside to let us in. Danny gives me a look that says *See?* This is going to be bad, too. When we pass the kitchen, Mrs. Fletcher looks up from her book and waves.

At the CAVE door, Warren enters his security code into the keypad and the lock *thunks*. "Don't touch anything."

"You sound like her," Danny says.

I give him a small shove, which isn't the nicest thing to do. Walking into the CAVE for the first time is a trip.

Literally.

With the walls painted black, and the dark carpet, you don't see the step down. Everyone trips the first time. It's like an initiation. After you trip *in* to the room, you trip out *on* the room.

Which is what Danny does.

Which makes Warren smile.

Which I interpret as we're off to a good start.

Warren shuts the door and I try to see the CAVE for the first time again, too. Black walls. Blackout curtains. DayGlo Milky Way painted across a ceiling populated by every known model of *Star Trek* spacecraft built to scale, hanging from wires. Saltwater fish tank in the far corner. Life-size Chewbacca behind the mountain of monitors, and a plasma ball glowing pink on the shelf above. Everywhere you look there's something techie, nerdy, cool. That's why Warren calls it the CAVE.

Coolness. Abounding. Virtually. Everywhere.

I note the absence of the Death Star he'd built out of poptops. It used to take up one whole corner of the ceiling. I can't believe he traded it for the constellation gun. Warren drank root beer until he barfed, collecting all those little tabs. Then he hung it like a menacing eye over his Warhammer Fantasy figurines. Those are all still on their table, lined up and ready for battle, black-lit so the whites of the Orcs' eyes glow.

Warren sits in the captain's chair by the computers. And Danny sinks into the beanbag by the door. I take the stool by the Warhammer table and fiddle with a wizard figurine.

"So." Warren tosses a Rubik's Cube between his hands. "Eevee tells me you have a problem."

"You could say that."

"And she thinks I can help."

"Hope so."

"But the question is . . ." Warren throws the cube up and watches it fall, spinning, into his hand. "Why should I?"

What is he doing? I set the wizard back on the table. "Warren . . ."

"Because here's the thing," he says, holding a hand up to me. "You laughed the loudest after you shut me in that locker."

Oh no.

Danny shakes his head. "That wasn't me."

"Yes, Eevee said that, too. Convenient, don't you think? Suddenly you're not responsible for being a total asswipe?"

"Warren, you said—"

"I'd help." He looks at me. "Yes. But what if he's just taking us for a ride?"

"Why would he make this up?"

Warren shrugs. "Have you asked him?"

I glare at Warren, then roll my eyes over to Danny. "Are you making this up?"

Danny looks incredulous. "You know I'm not."

"See?" I cross my arms. Warren tosses the cube again. And again. And again, until all I want to do is cram the stupid thing down his throat.

Danny breaks the tension. "What happened to you with the locker was wrong."

Warren stops tossing the cube.

"Listen, I don't know what to say or how to make you

believe me," Danny says, "but that wasn't me. I wouldn't have done that to you. The truth is, I don't remember ever seeing you before Monday morning."

Warren swivels back and forth in his chair, just staring at him, for a long, long time.

Time to get down to the business at hand. "Danny," I say, "tell Warren how you got here."

Danny clears his throat. "I was climbing over this fence—"

"Why?" Warren interrupts.

"Because I needed to get to the other side."

"What was over there?"

"A parking lot. Does it matter?"

"I don't know, does it?"

I sigh. "Warren, just let him tell the story." Warren holds his hands up in surrender, then goes back to flipping the cube.

"Let me start over." Danny sits forward and moves his hair out of his face. "It was Patriots' Day and there was a parade by the mall. Lots of people around. My friend and I were there on our skateboards. Suddenly there was an evacuation announcement over the sound system, and everyone scattered. Including me. There was a chain-link fence around the parking lot, and instead of finding another way around, I decided to go over it. So I'm climbing over and suddenly there's this huge explosion. Just massive. Then before I could even react, there was a second one, closer this time, that hit me like a wave. Everything went white. The force sent me flying and I landed hard. Smacked my head. It felt like my body was on fire. Then the ground sort of, I don't know, *gave way*. Like it just disappeared under me. I was falling and I thought, game over.

I'm a dead man. But then, next thing I know, I'm sitting at a desk. And she's there next to me."

"It was freaky," I add. "He gasped like he couldn't breathe."

Warren rests his chin on tented fingertips. "You said you hit your head. How do you know all of this isn't just some kind of amnesic episode?"

Danny shrugs. "It's possible, I guess."

"But *your* Phoenix isn't like this, right?" I ask.

"That's for sure." He runs his hands through his hair and closes his eyes. "I keep thinking maybe Red December had something to do with it."

This is new. "Who?"

Danny looks back and forth between us. "You know, the anarchist group. Car-bombed the Fed building downtown a few years ago? Hacked the stock exchange back in October? Tanked the market in minutes flat."

I can't believe what I'm hearing. From the look on Warren's face, he can't either. Danny climbs out of the beanbag and begins pacing.

"Who's the president?" Warren asks.

Danny makes a scoffing sound. "President? There hasn't been a president since my parents were kids. I mean, they have elections, but everyone knows they're just for show."

Warren leans forward, the Rubik's Cube forgotten in his hands. "So, who's in charge?"

"Coradetti. But it's pretty much agreed he's just a puppet." Danny stops pacing and looks at us. "You have a real president?"

The hair on my neck prickles. Warren swivels around in his

chair. "Okay," he says, his fingers typing on a keyboard. "Definitely not from around here."

"I tried that," Danny says. "Searching for answers. Didn't get anywhere."

Warren snickers. "This isn't Google. This is the Dark Web."

"Dark what?"

"Google it sometime."

"What's google?"

Warren stops typing. "Serious? Okay, never mind. Tell me about the explosion. Did you feel heat?"

Danny takes a step to look over Warren's shoulder. "A little. But it was more like getting shoved really hard. After, when I was lying there, I felt like my chest was gonna explode."

"Flash of light," Warren mutters. "Maybe it was some kind of dirty bomb." His fingers type like mad, then he punches one last key and turns around in his chair. "There. I posted a thread on the Outer Regions board. Maybe someone's heard of this Coradetti, or an explosion at a mall."

He swivels to face me. "Solomon, remember in 'Mirror, Mirror' when the Federation was replaced by an evil empire?"

"You mean Spock with the beard?"

"Yes."

"What about it?"

He points at Danny.

"You think Danny's been replaced by an evil empire?"

"Exactly. I mean, no. Well, sort of."

"What?" Danny asks.

I can feel my brain starting to cramp. "You're saying he's . . ."

Warren holds both hands palms down, side by side. "Parallel."

And that does it. My brain goes into gridlock. "But Mac says there's no way to cross between parallel worlds."

"Maybe Mac's wrong."

I laugh. "Mac? Wrong?"

Warren ignores me and pushes his goggles up onto his forehead. He's moved right from speculation to celebration. "Solomon, do you realize what this means? Can you fathom the implications if somehow he's slipped the bonds of space-time?"

I glance at Danny standing there confused out of his skull and think of what he'd said about the museum.

He's a different Danny.

Who kissed a different me.

16

DANNY

I try to break in, but they're locked on some scientific something I'm not even going to pretend I get. Eevee's eyes look like they're about to pop out of her head. Warren, though. He's all smiles. "This is huge, Solomon," he says. "Life-changing."

"Wait a second, guys." They're not listening.

"This could open the doors to the top colleges. Research labs. NASA. You name it."

"Wait," Eevee says.

Warren doesn't wait. "Heck, we'll be in demand on the international scene." He falls back into his chair and spins around like a kid.

"Wait a second!" I grab one of Warren's figurines, threatening to snap it in two.

That gets their attention. Eevee nods to Warren. "You explain it, Brainiac."

Warren hops up from the chair. "I'll make this simple. Try to keep up."

I hold out the action figure. Warren snatches it back and checks to make sure it isn't damaged before setting it down on a shelf.

"There's a theory—not proven yet, thus *theory*—that ours isn't the only universe." He clasps his hands behind his back and paces. "That there are, in fact, numerous universes, coexisting alongside ours. Together they're called a multiverse. Are you with me?"

"Yeah. Kind of."

"Okay. So in *theory*, quantum events spawn off new universes, creating parallel realities. The most famous example, of course, is Schrödinger's Cat."

"Whose cat?"

"Erwin Schrödinger. The physicist . . . ?" Warren pauses, apparently baffled by my lack of knowledge. He heaves a sigh as he explains. "Schrödinger suggested that if you put a cat in a box with a vial of poison gas and a trigger mechanism to release the gas if certain conditions are met, as long as the box remains sealed, the cat is both alive and dead *at the same time.*"

"Wait. I'm lost." I look at Eevee for help. "What does a cat in a box have to do with me being here?"

"What he's saying is, when there's a decision point—say, someone getting sick—that point branches the universe into two, one for each outcome. So in the example of the sick person, in one universe the person gets better, and in the other, the person doesn't."

"So the universe branched, and now there are two Phoenixes?"

Eevee shrugs. "Or more."

Warren jumps in again, talking excitedly in my face. "The number isn't what's important here. It's the fact that you traveled from your universe to ours."

Sometimes when Warren's excited, he spits when he talks. I take a step back. "And that part—the traveling bit—that's not supposed to happen?"

"Not according to the laws of physics." Eevee sits down again on the stool. "There aren't any known connection points between universes."

"There is now." Warren smiles.

"No," Eevee says.

"What do you mean, no?"

"He's a person, Warren."

"Of course he's a person."

"We have to be careful here. We can't say anything to anyone."

"Not even Mac?"

Eevee stares hard at Warren, drumming her fingers on her knee, thinking.

"Eevee," Warren whines, "we have to tell Mac."

Finally, she nods. "Okay. But only Mac. And we tell him together."

"After class tomorrow?"

"Deal."

Despite not understanding most of what they said, I'm hopeful. This feels like the first step toward getting back home. And that is the best news all day.

17

EEVEE

I push Dad's door open, and Danny follows me inside. He's happier than I've ever seen him—either as this self or his other self. He's talking nonstop about how he can't wait to get back to his family and all the things he'll tell them when he gets there, about this Phoenix and the foster home and about me. I don't have the heart to remind him all we have is a theory, not an instruction manual for somehow transporting him back home.

We walk into the kitchen and I pull a bag of veggie puffs from the cabinet. The bag crinkles open. I hold it out and sing the jingle. *"Muncha buncha puffs, the puffs made only from good stuffs."*

Danny takes a handful. I eat one, then another, and try to shake the unsettled feeling sweeping over me.

"Did you understand all that stuff?" He crunches a puff.

"Most of it."

"I knew you were smart," he says, "but dang. It was like

you guys were speaking another language." He goes on and on about how he thought he was decent at science but never learned any of the stuff we talked about at Warren's and . . . and . . . and . . . Then he stops talking and asks, "Are you okay?"

I look down at my hands and realize I'm strangling the Muncha Puffs bag.

I'm not okay.

"If this is true," I say, "we're talking a total game changer. If you really are from a parallel universe, then what happened to you could happen to any of us. Somehow you crossed from there to here. What's to stop that from happening to me? Or Warren? What does that mean for the stability of our universe?"

He's silent. He clearly doesn't have the answers either. I continue.

"And what about the other Danny? The one who usually lives here. Where is he now? And what if word about this gets out? If we're not careful, you could end up a lab rat. You saw the look in Warren's eyes. Don't think for a minute he won't sell you out. Danny Ogden, you are the missing link in the unified theory."

His jaw is set tight, his bubble burst. I hold out the bag. "More?" He shakes his head, so I put the Muncha Puffs back in the cupboard, then straighten the dish towel by the sink.

All of those things I said are true. All of them are huge problems, so big they could swallow us whole. But they're not what's really bothering me.

What's really bothering me is her.

The other Eevee.

She's the creeping feeling I can't shake, though I don't know why. I again straighten the towel that doesn't need straightening. "My dad'll be home soon. I should probably go get my homework done."

"Wait," he says, leaning against the kitchen counter. "Can I ask you something first?"

"Sure." I brace for another bombshell.

He shakes his head so all that hair falls in his face. "Will you cut this off?"

"What?" Okay, I totally didn't see that one coming. "No. No way."

"I can't take one more day of this shit hanging in my face." He blows a strand away from his mouth.

"Why don't you ask my dad when he gets home. There's a QuickCuts over on 51st. He can drive."

"I was thinking you could just do it."

"I don't know how."

"You'll figure it out."

"I'll make you look like a freak."

"Eevee . . ." He musses the hair and makes a face.

He has a point.

I hear myself say okay. Watch myself pull a towel out of the linen closet and scissors from the bathroom cabinet. They're small and sharp. They'll do the trick.

He sits in a chair in the middle of the kitchen with the towel around his shoulders, his hair hanging down over his face. I walk around him three or four times.

"What are you waiting for? Chop. Chop."

I laugh to cover the fear. "No pressuring the artist while she works."

"Oh, excuse me, Monet."

"Better Monet than van Gogh." I snap the scissors twice by his ear and he ducks.

I have no idea where to start. I've never cut anyone's hair before. Well, that's not entirely true. I chopped off my Barbies' hair when I was little. Those poor dolls looked tragic when I was finished with them. "You're sure about this?"

"Sure as I am about anything."

"That's not saying a whole lot."

I pull the comb through his mop. It's longer than I realized. Rattier, too. "Have you *ever* had your hair cut?"

"This isn't my hair, remember? I keep mine short."

Of course he does. In his universe.

I start small and slow, taking a few inches off the back at the center. The scissors make a sizzle noise as they slice through the strands. I'm holding my breath. I think he's holding his, too.

With my foot, I slide a couple of locks along the floor into his view. "Nervous?"

"No."

"Liar."

I take the length up to his collar. At least four or five inches more. The hair falls to the floor without a sound. I cut all around the bottom, trying to keep it even. The result: a slightly crooked bob. It's hard not to laugh, it looks so bad.

I step back to study the shape of his head and also to buy

time. Then I cut the bob shorter, to just below his ears. This is far worse than the Barbies.

I keep going, though. I keep the scissors cutting, taking off more and more until finally something like a rhythm kicks in. I lose myself in the work. Instead of combing the hair down his neck, I drag the comb up, stopping just above the hairline, and chop. Drag it up again and chop more. Snip, snip go the scissors. Down, down falls the hair. The floor is a mess. I'll have to clean it all up before Dad gets home or he'll freak out.

Soon jagged angles emerge. Tufts here and there, some long, some short. I don't worry about lines, matching lengths or any of those things professionals do. I just fight my way through. Move his head as I need to without apology.

"You're enjoying this."

He's right, but I don't tell him.

So, if careers in science or welding fail me, I'll be a hair-dresser. Maybe Mom's magazines are getting through to me. "Close your eyes."

"You really don't have any idea what you're doing, do you?"

"This was your brilliant idea, not mine."

He closes those blue eyes and I snip a slight angle across the bridge of his nose. The hair falls away from his face.

"Who's Mac?"

"Marcus McAllister. Teacher at Palo Brea. Probably the smartest man in the world. He used to be a NASA engineer."

"Can he help us?"

"Maybe. Hopefully."

"You trust him?"

"Yes."

He shifts his weight and tucks his hands between his knees. "I found them, you know."

"Who?"

"My parents."

"What? That's great! Why didn't you tell me?" I swoop his bangs out of his eyes. Then I see his face and understand.

18

DANNY

"Tell me about them," she says softly.

I'm looking at her face but all I see is the grave. Their names. The infinity symbol. I shake the image away and picture them instead at home. "Dad works for the city, at least he did, in infrastructure and planning. Mom volunteers part-time with kids. Helps them with reading."

But what they do isn't who they are. Nothing I say will recreate them. They're not here. She'll never meet them. If I at least had a picture, that would . . .

"Who do you take after?" She steps close again and works on my hair. My head feels about eighty pounds lighter. And I can see.

"Most people say my mom. My eyes are definitely hers, but my nose is more like Dad's."

She looks at my face. "I'm trying to imagine them."

I am, too. Friday morning before I left for Germ's, Dad was already off to work and Mom was just getting her coffee.

I yelled goodbye to her from the door. Didn't give her a hug. "They're older. Mom has a degenerative muscle condition that should have kept her from having kids. Doctors didn't think either of us would live. She says I was a feisty baby, though. Calls me her miracle boy."

"I like that," Eevee says, moving to stand behind me. "Miracle boy."

In my mind, I see Mom as she was that morning, standing by the kitchen counter, one hand on her cane. Red December blew up the mall. Did they hit other targets, too? Targets closer to home? I wish there was some way to know.

"Hope they're okay," I whisper. She touches my shoulder and I feel my eyes well up. Good thing she can't see my face. Time to change the subject. "What about your parents?"

She grunts. "You've met them. What's left to say?"

"The two-houses thing is pretty interesting."

"Weird, you mean. But it works, I guess."

"How old were you when they got divorced?"

"They were never married, actually." She moves in front of me again. "They liked each other enough at some point, but decided they were better off living as neighbors instead of like normal people. From what they've told me—which isn't much—having a kid was a matter of logic. Necessity. They're both only-children. It was important to them to keep their DNA chains around. So here I am." She laughs. "The archive."

"Wow. That's really . . ."

"Weird. I make it sound worse than it is. I mean, they're fine. They love me. They don't beat me or anything." She gasps, and a hand flies to her mouth. "I'm so sorry."

It takes me a second to make the connection. "It's okay. It's the other Danny you'd be apologizing to." What's crazy is I'd pretty much forgotten about the foster family. "So, how's it look?"

She sweeps my bangs to one side and then back. "Bizarre."

"Bizarre, but better?"

"Getting there." She steps around behind me again and combs through what's left of The Hair. "Actually . . . Hang on."

She rushes off and returns just as quickly with a container of green goop, which she slicks through my hair.

"So, if I'm here, who took my place there?" I try to picture some other me, living in my house, sleeping in my bed. "They'd notice if he's different, right?"

"You're different than the other Danny."

"My parents must be totally freaked-out."

"Your girlfriend, too."

"No girlfriend." I look at her out the corner of my eye. "Boyfriend?"

She scoffs. "As if." Then circles around to my right side. Her voice goes quiet. "Tell me about her."

"Who?"

"Eevee Solomon."

I exhale, choosing what to say. "Her hair is long and dark, like yours. Same eyes. Same smile." What I don't say: great kisser, legs impossibly long. I close my eyes, reliving that night again in my mind. "I hardly know her, but when I met her, it's like I wanted time to stop."

I feel a hand on my shoulder and open my eyes. She's looking at me intently, her hair falling around her face. I reach up, tuck one side behind her ear, let my fingers touch her jaw. Her lips part and a smile tugs the corner of her mouth.

Then she blinks and inhales. Lifts her hand from my shoulder. "I . . ." Her voice cracks. She steps back, sets the scissors on the counter and walks toward the door.

"Eevee, wait."

She doesn't stop, though. Doesn't even turn. The door closes and she's gone.

19

EEVEE

He calls my name, but I let the door shut behind me and walk-run back home. Mom's sitting at the computer with her phone to her ear. She doesn't see me.

Just like he didn't see me. Not really. He was looking into my eyes, but in his mind he was seeing her.

Why does that bother me?

I slam the door, flop onto my bed and curl up on my side. My heart pounds in my ears.

The idea of me and Danny is absurd. Nothing good would come of us being together. That's the truth of the matter. Just look at Mom and Dad.

When I was a kid—maybe four or five years old—I watched my parents dancing. I don't remember where we were, and I've never asked. I don't want them to spoil it. In my memory, there are trees with twinkling lights and candles on tables. Mom's dress swishes around as she and Dad sway in circles. He holds her right hand like it's a delicate thing, and his left arm is wrapped around her waist. He tucks her hand against his chest and she rests her chin on his shoulder. Their eyes are closed.

They were together. They were happy. And now look at them, ten years later.

Who's to say the same thing wouldn't happen to me and Danny. If.

I roll on my back and stare at the ceiling.

Still, it would be nice for him to look at me like that, the way he looks at the other Eve.

Enough. This is stupid. I have work to do.

I push myself off the bed, tuck in my earbuds and douse my brain with Bach. Time to get busy. Time to review those physics notes. I read Faraday's law of induction from the textbook out loud.

"'The induced electromotive force in any closed circuit is equal to the negative of the time rate of change of the magnetic flux through the circuit.'"

Three times I read it, but the words are just noise. I close my eyes and see him looking at me, feel his hand touching my face.

Focus, Eevee. You need to get this. You need to nail the grades, lock in the GPA, make it into the right college, the right research-assistant position. Then you'll land the right job and . . .

I read the definition two more times, enunciating every word.

Land the right job and then . . . And then what?

Dad says a relationship would be an unnecessary distraction from finals and college-entrance exams. It would only get in the way of my goals.

I read through the first sentence again, but end up staring at the wall. How does that feel, liking someone so much you want time to stop? Those were his words.

About me.

Only, not me.

I bend the corner of the textbook up and down. Why is this bothering me so much? I need to just let it go. Buckle down and do what's expected of me. So I can go places. And accomplish stuff.

Alone.

I slam the textbook shut and slide it off the desk. It lands on the carpet with a thud.

I want him to feel that way about me.

It's irrational. Stupid.

But it's the truth.

20

DANNY

From the kitchen, I hear the front door open. My hands work faster, trying to clean up the mess. The paper towels make swishing sounds as I sweep them across the floor. In my mind, I rehearse what I'll tell Sid about what happened here.

But it isn't Sid who walks into the room.

It's Eevee.

She tears paper towels from the roll and joins me on the floor. Together we gather up the hair, reaching around the edges of the cabinets and the legs of the chair.

I turn around, still on my hands and knees, and she's there again, in front of me, looking at me with those eyes. I smile. "You came back."

"I came back."

I move closer and lean in, afraid I'm going to scare her off again. But she doesn't pull away. Her eyes are wide, her lips, so close.

The front door opens.

Sid's home from work.

21

EEVEE

First thing Wednesday morning Warren and I dash to Mac's room, hoping to catch him before class and tell him about Danny. But instead of Mac, we're greeted by Mr. Rubino, Mac's go-to substitute.

"Sorry," he says, writing notes on the whiteboard. The green marker squeaks as it forms each word. "Mr. MacAllister is at the ACE conference today and tomorrow."

"Fail," Warren groans.

The first students begin filtering in. Mr. Rubino recaps the marker and shuffles his lecture notes. "I'm sure whatever it is, it can wait until he gets back."

"Here's hoping." I grab Warren by the sleeve.

Outside the room we synchronize our watches, so to speak. One of Warren's Dark-Web contacts—Captain Kaboom—suggested the explosion generated an EMP that created a shockwave that pushed Danny through to our universe. It didn't sound likely, but since Warren and I know next to nothing about electromagnetic pulses or radiation, we decided research was in order.

"Library at lunch?" I hold out my fist.

"Library. Lunch." He bumps it.

The first bell rings and we part ways.

●

Warren groans as he scrolls through the search results on the library computer. "Over 500,000."

I check the clock. We have twenty minutes until our next class. "Where do we start?"

"Wiki, I guess." He clicks the first link and we wait. The library computers are super slow. Across the shelves, I can just see Danny's shoulder. The page finally loads.

"About time," Warren says. He scrolls as we read.

"Produces damaging current and voltage surges," I whisper.

"Looks like this is mostly about high-altitude EMPs." He clicks the back button. "From what Parallel Boy said, this happened at ground level."

"Nothing about the effects on humans either."

He clicks another link that leads to a particularly ugly site. The bright aqua background makes my eyes ache. "This one looks really technical."

The word *symptoms* catches my eye. "Wait."

Warren stops scrolling and we both lean closer to the monitor.

"What are you guys doing?"

We bolt upright in our seats. Missy is standing behind us, her braids hanging down the front of her shoulders. How long has she been there, listening? She tips her head to the right and peers beyond us at the computer.

"Research," I say, reaching for the mouse. Warren clicks the button first, dragging the browser window lower on the screen. The heading with the letters *EMP* stands out against the aqua. I scoot my chair over, hoping my shoulder will block her view.

"Research about what?" Her voice is like syrup. She sets her books down on the table beside us. We need to get rid of her before she makes herself comfortable. I look at Warren, but he's in a Missy stupor.

"Temperature variances in Phoenix over the last one hundred years." I tap Warren's foot with my own. "Right? Warren?"

"Phoenix," Warren says, "right." His face is flushed.

"Is that your science fair entry?"

"Yeah," I say, hoping she buys it.

She doesn't. Her face is incredulous. "Isn't that a bit rudimentary?"

"Well, it's just the start of a really, really big project with lots and lots of components that we don't have time to— Oh!" I point to the clock. "Speaking of the time, we need to get back to work now, don't we?"

Warren doesn't respond.

"I could help you, if you want." Missy smiles, then a big, goofy grin spreads across Warren's face. I'm surprised his goggles aren't steaming up, the way he's looking at her. He opens his mouth to respond to her offer, but I cut him off.

"No thanks. We've got it under control."

Her smile falls. "Fine." She hugs her books to her chest.

"I'll be over there studying, in case you change your mind. Bye, Warren."

Finally, she's gone.

"Earth to Warren." I snap my fingers in front of his face.

He blinks and his brain switches back on. "Huh? Oh."

"Nice to see you again. Can we get back to work now?" I check to make sure we're out of Missy's line of sight and pull the browser window back up. "Isn't harmful to humans," I read, "unless detonated near a hospital or individuals with electrical implants."

"Does he have a pacemaker?"

I look over at Danny, still by the shelves. "I have no idea."

"Whoa, cool." Warren points at the screen. "It says here the body fluids of someone with an electrical implant hit by microwaves would turn to steam and vaporize."

"That's horrific."

"Catching a reflection of the wave," he continues, "on a metal surface could cause severe burns and brain damage. Didn't Danny say he was holding on to a chain-link fence?"

He walks toward us, carrying a book in one hand and tossing an apple with the other.

I keep my voice low. "Brain damage, Warren? Really?"

"It says so right here."

"He does not have brain damage."

Danny drops the book on the table and sets the apple on top.

I turn the book to read the title. "*Beyond the Street: The 100 Leading Figures in Urban Art.* I'm surprised they let that book in here."

"You don't have a pacemaker, do you?" Warren asks.

"That's random. No."

"Warren thinks you have brain damage."

"I didn't say . . ."

Danny scrunches up his face and starts twitching, his tongue out and arms scrambled. Mrs. Colliard, the librarian, clears her throat and gives us the evil eye.

"I didn't say you had brain damage," Warren mutters under his breath.

"I've been told worse." Danny rolls the apple back and forth across the table. "So you guys figure anything out?"

I shake my head, but Warren says, "One thing. We know what we're doing for our science project."

"We do?"

"The effects of EMPs on humans."

"No." I hold up my hands. "We are not studying him."

"Of course we are," Warren says. "We've already begun."

"He's not a lab rat."

"No one said he was."

Mrs. Colliard clears her throat again. I lower my voice to a growl. "That's what it'll lead to."

"Why do you think that?" He crosses his arms but keeps his voice down. "Be logical, Solomon. We figure out what's up with him and we get our project done. If we discover something amazing along the way, like parallel transport, we also win the science fair. Oh, and *change the face of science.*"

I cross my arms, too. "He can't be involved."

Danny stops rolling the apple. "Why not?"

"Because we can't draw attention to you." I turn back to

Warren. "What are we going to do? Build our own EMP device? Who's not being logical now?"

"Will it help solve whatever's going on with me?"

"Maybe it will generate a shock wave that will push you back to your own universe," Warren says.

"Then do it. I'm your lab rat."

I protest. "But—"

"No worries. If it helps, awesome. If it doesn't, then nothing's changed." Danny tosses the apple and catches it. "Now who's being logical?"

"You didn't consider the third outcome." I keep my voice even.

"What's that?"

"We really do give you brain damage."

"Oh." He takes a bite of the apple. "Yeah, that would suck."

It turns out Danny is really good at English. I have the proof in my bag. Last night after the haircut, he helped me rewrite my essay. Then we sat outside and talked until we were both yawning and Dad had to flash the porch light to signal it was time for me to go home.

The Fish's belly has grown gargantuan, and with it her crankiness. She scowls when Danny and I enter the room. We made it to class just before the late bell. A first for Danny. She seems more annoyed that he's there on time than she ever was when he was late.

I sit down, tap Kyle's leg and brush Sarah's hair off my

desk. Sarah turns around again and again to look at Danny. Each time, her hair falls back on my desk. A few more students walk in late and The Fish leaps into her usual tirade about what awful students we are and how many days she has before her maternity leave. As if we aren't counting down, too.

"Those of you who had to rewrite your essays may put them on my desk now," she grumbles. "Meanwhile, I'll be passing around the review packet for the test."

I pull my sparkly new essay out of my bag and smile at Danny. I have to wait for The Fish to waddle past before going up front and adding it to the stack. Seems I'm not the only one who hadn't met her standards.

When I get back to my desk, Sarah's whispering something to Danny. I break through their conversation to sit down. She raises her hand. "Ms. Fish—uh—Fischbach? Danny doesn't have a book. Can I share mine with him?"

The Fish, annoyed at the disruption, glares at Danny. "If it is your intention to take initiative in this class, Mr. Ogden, you will need your textbook. For now, you may look on with Sarah. *If* you remain quiet."

Sarah beams, but then Danny asks, "Is it okay if I look on with Eve?" and her mouth falls into a pout.

The Fish waves a hand—"Fine, fine"—and continues to pass out review sheets.

Sarah swishes her hair and turns away. Kyle grunts and unwinds his feet from my desk. I scoot toward Danny, glad to be free of both the stink and the jiggle. If only I could be free of The Fish.

I open my textbook and set it on the spot where our desks

touch. The tissue-thin pages crinkle as he turns to the first story listed on the review sheet, "The Story of an Hour," by Kate Chopin. We work side by side, pointing out the answers for each story and filling out the sheet. When we get to "The Open Boat," he grabs my paper, flips it over and starts drawing. I watch, amazed, as he pencils the lines of a pirate ship, shading in the billowing sails and Jolly Roger. Waves crash against the figurehead and ripple along the prow. He hands the paper back to me and returns to his review sheet like nothing happened.

I tap his foot, and mouth *Wow.* He shrugs. The Fish clears her throat and we get to work on "The Yellow Wall-Paper." That story freaked me out, a woman locked up and losing her mind, seeing things in the walls. I snatch Danny's packet, flip it over and use the edge of my own packet to draw the first line at a 37-degree angle. Then I close my eyes and see the rest of the fractal bloom, a flower of numbers and lines sprouting with mathematical precision, each new section materializing as a perfect replica of the one that came before. My hand goes to work, transferring the image in my mind onto the paper before I even open my eyes.

When the fractal is done, I hand the packet to him and focus on "The Yellow Wall-Paper."

He taps my foot, but I ignore him, trying not to smile as I search out answers in the book. He taps my foot again. When I don't respond, he bumps me hard with his leg. WOW is scribbled across the top of his paper. He draws a circle around the word and adds an exclamation point. I shrug.

Sarah's had enough of our fun. "They're distracting me," she whines, her finger pointing at us, revenge in her eyes.

I feign innocence. "We're just doing our work."

The Fish makes a big production of getting out of her chair and waddling over to our desks with one hand supporting her lower back. Everyone watches her pick up my review packet first, then Danny's. She flips through the pages, turns them over, turns them sideways and cocks her head to the right. Without a word, she tears both packets in two.

"You." She points at Danny. "Out."

"You." She points at me. "Put your desk back and stay silent the rest of the class."

She mutters all the way back to her desk.

"Later." Danny struts across the room and slams the door behind him.

Sarah flips her hair across my desk. Kyle tucks his feet in and jiggles my chair. Crap. I need that review if I'm going to pass the test.

After an eternity, class ends and I walk up to The Fish's desk, holding my books like a shield.

"What?" She looks disgusted to have me so close.

"May I have a new copy of the review sheet, please?"

She purses her lips and exhales through her nose before reaching into her desk.

"May I please have one for Danny, too?"

"He won't pass the class."

"You never know."

She hands me a second packet.

"Thank you." I head for the door.

"Miss Solomon."

I force myself to turn and look at her.

"Though English is not your strongest suit, I'm told you

have great potential as a student. I suggest you take better care in choosing your friends."

Instead of telling her off, I thank her and leave.

At the opposite end of the walkway between the English and history classrooms, I see Missy talking to Principal Murray. Whatever she's telling him, she's pretty animated about it. Her braids bob and her hands punctuate the air. He seems to mostly watch the students passing by, though, stopping one for running, another for littering. I wish I were close enough to hear what they were talking about. Danny materializes at my side. "You survived."

"Barely. Look. New review packets."

"I'm not going back in that room."

"But—"

"Nope. No way I'm going to be pushed around by that woman again."

"You'll fail."

"Don't care." He saunters down the sidewalk. "In fact, why don't we just leave this place?"

I hurry to catch up to him. "What do you mean? We can't do that."

"Why?"

"We'll get caught."

"And then what?"

"My dad will kill me."

He tucks his hands into his pockets and looks at the sky. "You'd be surprised how people don't actually notice when you're gone." We've almost reached the end of the sidewalk. "The secret is not making a big deal about it."

The second bell rings. We keep walking.

"Just tell yourself no one can see you and they won't." He steps off the curb into the parking lot and I follow, trying to convince myself I'm invisible.

We walk through the gate and—like that—we're ditching school.

I'm ditching school, something I would never do.

But another me might.

"This way." He turns right and takes the road leading south. "I want to show you something."

22

Danny

I kind of feel guilty, but not too much. The sun is shining and there's a pretty girl beside me. We walk out of the school and I'm amazed again at how easy everything is here.

"No, really," she says. "What do I do when I get caught?"

"You tell them you were sick in the bathroom."

"They won't believe that."

I walk backward to face her. "Sure they will. You're a good student. They'll trust anything you say. And Danny, well . . ." I turn back around. "No one cares if he's gone or not, right?"

I can tell she doesn't believe me.

"We'll go back in a bit, okay? Promise."

She bites her lip, but nods and shifts the bag on her shoulder.

"Want me to carry that?"

"No, I've got it."

We walk side by side. The only sounds are the garbage trucks picking up cans, and dogs barking behind fences. Halfway down the block, I stop.

"The best I can tell, this is where I was skating that morning," I say, pointing to where we're standing. "There are some restaurants and shops over here, and a winding road that wraps around that way. And over there." I turn around. "That whole area there is the mall. Or was."

I can tell she's trying to envision it. If only I could somehow transfer the images from my brain to hers. Make her see my world.

"The fence I climbed would be somewhere over this way." I walk farther down the sidewalk, imagining the people lined up to see the parade. The strip mall of shops. The smoking woman and ShopMart at the end. Eevee follows, listening as I tell her more about that morning. I look around at the houses with their gravel-and-cactus yards, the mailbox flags raised, letters ready for pickup. A woman shuffles her garbage can toward the curb.

We cross the street and walk onto the greens of the Bel Air Country Club. A couple of golfers watch us, two ratty kids interrupting their game. One tees off, and I yell, "Eight!"

She laughs. "Isn't it 'fore'?"

"But there are two of us." She gives me a look. "Oh, all right." I yell again. "Four!"

A golfer waves us on and we walk through to the other side of the course.

"Tell me about Germ," she says. "What's he like?"

Ducks swim in the water trap, quacking at each other. Every now and then one quacks really loud. Sounds like he's laughing. I close my eyes and see Germ skating away, the gym bag of supplies slung over his shoulder. Maybe he made it out.

Maybe the blast only threw him like it threw me. Maybe it didn't reach him at all.

I swallow down my doubt, and think instead about all the insane antics we've gotten away with over the years. Building things just to burn them down. Pushing the boundaries as far as they could go. Not because we were looking for trouble, but because we were curious. What would happen if? What would it be like if? From that day we met in second grade, we were inseparable. Two kids with big ideas and just enough guts—or lack of brains—to give them a try.

When I open my eyes, the impossible golf course faces me again. I don't trust my voice. "Hard to put Germ into words. Like a brother."

She nods like she gets it, but how can she? Can anyone?

"We're street artists." I shove my hands in my pockets and start walking again. Moving makes it easier to talk.

"Do you mean, like, graffiti?"

"No. I mean, like, art."

"But that's illegal."

I shrug.

"Is it illegal where you're from?"

"It breaks compliance laws. But we find ways to do it anyway."

"Is that where you learned your invisibility trick?"

I grin.

"Sounds like you have such a great life there," she says. "Your parents . . . Germ . . ."

"You'd think so, right?" We wait for a car to pass and then cross another busy street. "But in my world, you can't ever let your guard down. You're always being watched. Listened to. Speak out about the wrong thing and you end up on someone's shit list. Make a wrong move and you're done. If anyone has it good, Eevee, it's you." I hold my hands out and turn in a circle. "Look around. The sun is shining and you are free to do whatever you want."

"Are you sure you want to go back there?"

I don't hesitate. "Of course. It's home." And then I have an idea. "Let me show you one more thing and then we'll go back, okay?"

She agrees.

Our shoes shuffle along the sidewalk. The sun warms our backs as we cross the street and walk into the neighborhoods. After a while of just being quiet, she asks, "What happened that things went so bad there?"

"Well . . ." I run a hand through my hair and try to figure out where to start. "A long time ago, the Soviet Union launched a satellite into space."

"Sputnik?"

"You've heard of it?"

"Of course."

"Okay, well, Sputnik caused a lot of problems between the US and the Soviets. They got into a kind of pissing contest, each side scrambling to build bigger, better weapons to outgun the other guy. They also created new ways of spying on each other. Things got really tense when the Soviets planted nukes in Cuba. Suddenly the enemy was right at the doorstep. So the government created a system to track the bad guys, in case they found a way inside. It worked so well, they decided to keep it going, even after Cuba backed off. There was always a new threat, a new enemy. So they kept upgrading the system. Expanding it. Eventually they gave it the name Spectrum."

"You've mentioned that a couple of times."

"It's awful. A mix of technology and old-fashioned brute force. You never know how you're being tracked. Avoid the cameras, but the guy behind you in line might be listening. I've heard rumors they're working on a new upgrade. Spectrum 2.0."

"That's really scary."

"And effective. Most people are scared of stepping out of line. Others have just gotten used to living with it. Every now and then you hear about a protest or a conflict somewhere, but they stamp those out pretty quickly."

"Like Red December?"

"Exactly."

"How bizarre. Our Cold War ended when they tore down the Berlin Wall."

"Ours didn't end. It turned into an ice age."

We follow the road as it curves into Pascal. "There." I point to the brown house that should be blue. A camping trailer sits in the driveway instead of a boat. "That one's mine. Except we have a huge eucalyptus tree growing in the front. Sheds like crazy. Dad's always asking me to rake up the mess."

"Why do you keep doing that?" she asks.

"What?"

"Touching the collar of your shirt."

I realize my hand is at my neck, reaching for what isn't there. "My mom gave me a necklace when I was a kid. I must have lost it."

"No," she says, "the other Danny is wearing it now."

"That makes sense." I look again at my should-be house. "I keep thinking maybe if I stand here long enough they'll walk out the front door."

She touches my arm. "It's okay. You're going to see them again. We'll figure out a way."

She doesn't sound very sure, but I let myself believe. She lifts the strap of her bag and resets it on her shoulder. Her neck is red where it's been rubbing.

"Please, let me carry that."

This time she doesn't argue. I put it on my shoulder and pretend to stumble under the weight. "Too many books!"

She laughs and we retrace our steps back to the school.

23

EEVEE

When I wake, I'm tangled in the sheets, my heart racing and my legs trying to run from falling bombs and cracks in my walls. I tell myself it's just a dream, but I reach out and touch the wall to make sure it's solid. When I was little and got scared, I would listen for my dad snoring. I knew if I could hear him, everything was okay. But I'm not little anymore, and it's hard to hear Dad when he lives next door.

I untangle myself and wander down the hall. Morning sun streams in through the kitchen window. Mom looks up from her coffee and paper.

"Sleep didn't help?"

When we'd returned to campus the day before, I'd gone straight to the nurse and told her I felt sick. I couldn't look her in the eye, so I covered my face and mumbled something about my head hurting. Between ditching and hearing Danny's stories, I was such a mess she had no problem believing me.

Mom believed me, too. She touches the back of her hand to my forehead. "You don't feel warm. Want some toast? Juice?"

She sees the answer on my face. "I'll call the school. You go lie down."

The couch catches my fall. The weatherman smiles. His skin is so tan it's orange. "Gorgeous day today. Sunshine and a high of 76°."

I listen to mom leaving a message on the attendance line. "This is Judy Bennett. My daughter, Eve Solomon, will be out sick today."

"Don't forget the homework!"

"Please have her homework ready for me to pick up this afternoon. Thanks." Mom walks into the room and mutes the television. "I'm sorry I can't be home to take care of you. I have appointments all day. Remember to eat something if you can. And call me if you get to feeling really bad, okay?"

I groan.

"Go back to bed."

I groan again and shuffle to my room.

The plan goes off without a hitch. I stay in my room until Mom is gone, then check the windows to make sure Warren has moved on and Dad's car is no longer in the drive. The EMP discussion is on hold until Mac gets back tomorrow, and Danny has things he wants to show me. No time like the present, right? Still, my hands shake as I get dressed and slip out through the backyard.

Danny is waiting for me in the alley. A duffel bag hangs from the handlebars of a bike.

"Didn't think you had it in you."

"I guess you don't know me very well. Where'd you get this?"

"I bought it at a garage sale the other day with some of Danny's money. Like it?"

"Sure." I hold on to his shoulders and step onto the pegs sticking out from the back tire. He pedals and we're off.

The orange-skinned weatherman was right. It's a beautiful day. I lift my face to the sun. I don't know me very well either.

I have no idea where we're going, and I don't ask. Danny rides in the street, heading south through the neighborhood, passing houses and cars and women watering their lawns. Dogs bark and sprinklers run into the gutter. I hold on and try to keep my feet from slipping. When we reach Thunderbird Road, he turns right and we ride with the traffic. The wind whips through my hair and Danny's shoulders grow warm beneath my hands. Every now and then he says something, but I can't hear him over the noise. Soon houses give way to strip malls and block walls and I lose track of time. My legs grow tired, standing on the pegs.

"Almost there?" I yell. I can't hear his answer, but see him nod.

At 59th Avenue Danny ditches the main road for a shortcut through a parking lot. Drive-Thru Liquor and Forever Fitness whir by before he turns around the far side of the Flower Shack. We coast down a sloped path leading into Paseo Park. I've seen it from the road a number of times. From the Thunderbird overpass it doesn't look like anything special, but down inside it's enormous. What once was a canal is now full of grass and trees, playgrounds and bike paths.

Danny rides under the overpass, taking me to a world I never knew existed.

I hop off the bike, still feeling the pegs in the arches of my feet, and look at the bridge above me. Every inch of the walls and ceiling is covered in graffiti.

"Yes! I knew it would be here." Danny throws his bag over his shoulder and climbs the sloped support of the overpass. I follow, trying to keep myself from slipping back down to the grass below.

He stops where the ceiling meets the wall. The traffic rumbles loudly over our heads. He sets the bag at his feet, then pulls out a pair of black gloves and a can of spray paint.

"Where did you get those?"

"Pinched them from the foster home." He flashes a wicked smile and goes to work. The aerosol can hisses as he sprays a line of black across the concrete.

"Danny." I check to see if anyone is watching.

"What?" More black lines turn into black boxes. He pulls another can from the bag and continues to work, his body angled and shoes gripping the concrete. The black boxes turn into a city skyline. Buildings with windows lit up in yellow.

The park is deserted and the traffic growls nonstop above. I take in the pictures around me. A Tyrannosaurus rex, red-eyed and salivating, snaps at a tangle of words, all sharp angles and indecipherable. The soft shades of a man's face and the letters *R, I* and *P* below. Psychedelic flowers in bright pinks and blues swirling around a whirlpool sun. A robot with a human skull. An octopus with bulging eyes and curlicue tongue, tentacles wrapped around the throat of King Kong. And all kinds of words. Block letters and scrolling letters and letters that look like shards of glass.

"Are any of these yours?"

"Nope. Haven't been out since I got here." He takes a moment to stretch his arms up over his head, then goes back to work. "I almost feel like me again."

The more I look, the more I notice the differences in each picture. The styles, the shading. With a little study, I'm able to decode the artists' names tucked into the edges. Buzz. Sweet Tooth. Sham. Big Boy. Vermin. And then I watch a new Danny emerge like the picture he's painting. His arm moves closer to the concrete and then back, closer and back, and his body moves rhythmically with him. The city buildings grow into spirals that swirl into an arm with ghostly black-and-blue fingers reaching back toward the buildings. Moving quickly, he draws a boy on top of a high-rise, running from the arm. The boy has long black hair and wears a black shirt and stoner high-tops. Around the curve of the menacing hand, he sprays the letters *D, O* and *A.*

His signature.

He stands back and wipes his forehead with his arm. "Wanna try?"

I shake my head so hard I almost slide down the wall.

"You sure?" He fishes through the bag and hands a glove to me. I pull it over my hand, my heart racing. He shakes the can and the clanking of the ball echoes off the concrete.

"What if . . ."

"What if nothing. Here." He hands me the paint. I turn the can over and read the label. Rust-Oleum. Deep blue. I take a breath, aim the can and spray a blue dot. Then another blue dot. Then a curved line beneath them. The paint runs down the slope. My smiley face looks like it's drooling.

He crosses his arms. "You can do better than that."

"Well, excuse me. I've never broken the law before."

"Let me help you." He stands behind me and extends his arm along mine. He's so close. The panic I felt while cutting his hair rises again, and with it the realization of what I'm doing. What I've done.

I should be in school. Not here. Not committing a crime.

I step away from him and hold out the can. "I can't do this."

He steps back, nodding. "It's okay." He takes the can and paints a moon over his cityscape with huge craters pocking the surface. As it takes form, I see how he's tucked my name into the design.

E V

24

Danny

She sits on the handlebars to give her feet a rest from the pegs. Her dark hair streams toward me. I let the wheels laze to the left and then to the right, pedaling just fast enough to keep us moving forward. She grips the bar and her laughter rises up to the sky.

No Spectrum. No checkpoints. Total freedom and perfect company. The sun is hot on my back and my leg muscles burn, but you couldn't pay me to be anywhere else.

"Do you know what time it is?" she yells.

"Nope." If it were up to me, I'd turn around, go back and paint more, or just find a place to hang. But I can tell she's starting to worry, so I pedal faster and focus on how the light shines on her shoulders. How she shakes her hair. I know we can't be late, but I also don't want to rush this.

I slow to a stop at 43rd Avenue. She shifts her weight and whines, "Ouch."

The crosswalk button squeaks when I press it. "Want to stand on the back again? Or you could drive."

"It's okay. I'm fine."

I look beyond her across the intersection. Back home, they've routed this road down to one lane, and every car gets searched. One of the permanent checkpoints.

The blinking crosswalk hand switches to the walking man and I pedal us out into the intersection. I watch the faces of the people waiting at the light. They're miserable. The man in the Civic talking on his cell phone. The one in the work truck, too, with his elbow on the window and his fingers tapping the frame. The woman looking in her rearview. Every single one looks like they'd rather be somewhere else.

They have no idea how it could be.

We're almost across the intersection when I can't take it anymore. "Hold the bike up." Eevee startles and hops down from the handlebars. I grab a paint can from the bag and shake it. The marble inside clangs against the metal.

"What are you doing?"

"Get over on the curb." I see the crosswalk sign counting down. Have to be quick. I run back to where the cars are waiting and start spraying on the road, using the sidewalk lines as a guide. That does the trick. Horns start blaring and I pray there aren't cops around.

I finish just as the light changes and run to where Eevee waits on the side of the road.

"What did you write? I couldn't see from here."

"Wake. Up." I grin.

She shakes her head. "You're insane."

"Now you say that like it's a good thing."

We turn onto her street. The house on the corner is a junk-fest and I dodge three mangy cats that dart across the road. Each house on the block is slightly nicer in a progression leading up to hers. Rusted-out cars to yards needing a mow to raked gravel to pristine. That corner house must make her dad crazy.

I swerve down the alley, retracing our morning route. When we reach the back of her house, I hold the bike steady while she climbs down. She unlatches the gate and I figure that's it. She'll go play sick for when her mom gets home and I'll go chill at her dad's. But she holds the gate open instead. I leave the bike in the alley and follow.

She peers through the back window. "I think we made it in time." She unlocks the door and I follow her inside, closing the door behind me.

Her mom's house is completely different from her dad's. The kitchen towels don't match, and one is crumpled up into the oven door handle. A bag of bread sits on the counter surrounded by crumbs. A stack of papers threatens to topple into a vase of wilting flowers. The TV is on in the living room and a blanket slouches across the couch.

"Welcome to sick bay." She clicks off an afternoon talk show, and then fiddles with the remote, turning it over in her hands.

Makes me nervous watching her. "I should go."

"No." She sighs. "I want to show you something."

"Okay."

"But . . . it's not something I let a lot of people see. No one, actually."

"You've got a body stuffed in the basement?"

"No." She laughs and leads me down the hallway. "The dead guy's no big deal."

We stop at what must be her bedroom, and my brain goes into overdrive. She unlocks the door and I follow her inside.

Once when I was little, my mom took me to this children's playhouse center. It was an old warehouse downtown, turned into a place for kids to run around and bounce off the walls. In one of the corners there was a huge black box. I didn't want to go in it, but Mom said I would like it and she led me by the hand. Stepping inside that black box was like stepping into space. It was dark, and there were tiny lights going on forever. Totally magical. Suddenly I was an astronaut, surrounded by stars. Mom couldn't get me to leave.

Stepping into Eevee's room feels like stepping into that black box. It's a vortex of colors and shapes. Like what she drew on the back of my paper in that horrible woman's class, only in color. Every inch of the place is covered in spiraling designs, shaded in pinks, greens and blues.

"Eevee, this is . . ."

"They're fractals," she says, her hands clasped in front of her. She stares at the ceiling. "Scientists say the universe is built in fractals. I created these using different equations. That one there is similar to the Koch curve."

It's like she's speaking Greek, but it doesn't matter. I'm in awe, almost like I've crossed worlds again.

She keeps talking, really fast. "It's just a repetitive math-ematical process, really. Start with a line and figure the angle based on its trajectory, then repeat the process, allowing the equation to determine the curve and complexity of the design. The one starting there by the window is kind of interesting. I used the Fibonacci sequence, which of course is the same pattern found throughout the natural world. See how it kind of resembles the center of a sunflower?"

"This must have taken forever."

"It's just something I've done for as long as I can remember. Everywhere I look, I see rays and angles and I can't help but figure out their patterns. When things start feeling really big and out of control, fractals remind me how to get back to simple."

"That's amazing."

She shrugs. "They're just patterns. The mathematical equivalent of bubble gum. Something to chew on, to see how far it stretches."

"Call it whatever you want. It's art."

"Well, it's certainly nothing practical."

"Do they make you feel something?"

She thinks for a moment. "Yes."

"Then screw practical."

"Practical pays for college." Sounds like her dad. Then she cocks her head to the side. "Isn't it strange that we both draw on walls?"

I mimic her and cock my head to the side, too. "Isn't drawing on the walls what crazy people do?"

"Cavemen drew on walls."

"Yeah, well, cavemen were totally crazy, running around trying to invent fire so they could grill dinosaur steaks."

"Dinosaur steaks?" She makes a face, then realizes I'm

messing with her and rolls her eyes. I move toward one wall to get a closer look at the work. I see her reflection in the mirror on the closet door, then step forward to capture us both in the frame. Our eyes meet and everything stands still. Just the two of us suspended in a world of colors and angles—a world of her own making.

"Eve?" Her mom's voice coming down the hall shatters the magic.

She gasps, locks the door and completely freaks out. Messes up her bed. Looks in the mirror and messes up her hair. Pushes me out of the way while she does a silent spaz. Before she blows a gasket, I catch her by the arms, hold her still, look her in the eye. "Does your window have screens?"

She nods.

"Is there another back door?"

"Mom's room."

"Perfect. I'll hide so you can distract her, then I'll sneak out the door. Piece of cake."

She looks scared.

"Trust me."

She nods, but the lines across her forehead tell the truth.

"Hey." I look up at the ceiling and then into her eyes. "Thank you for showing me this." Then I kiss her on the lips, real quick before she steps away.

Her mom knocks on the bedroom door. "Eve?"

I sneak into the closet, leaving her standing there, stunned.

25

EEVEE

He kissed me.

Mom knocks on the door again. "Eve? Are you in there?"

"Yeah." My voice cracks. I stumble around like I'm not in control of my own body. "Just a sec."

"I've got your homework and some things to help you feel better."

"Be right out."

The closet door looms over me. I have to stay cool. I can't mess this up.

But he kissed me.

Kissing is supposed to happen to other girls. Girls like Stacy Farley. Not girls like me.

My hands shake as I reach for the bedroom door. By the time I get it open, Mom is already at the other end of the house. I close it behind me without letting it latch.

In the living room, I flop onto the couch and curl up, my heart pounding in my head.

"There you are." Mom feels for my temperature. "You're clammy."

"I feel better than this morning."

"Well, you look worse."

She hands me my homework and walks to the kitchen. "I thought a stir-fry might be good tonight. I got that sauce you like so much. But maybe soup would be better? Oh, and look in the bag on the chair. Got you some new magazines."

I check the back windows. Where is he?

"Which do you want?" Mom asks. I dash back to the couch before she returns to the living room. "I can make either."

And then I see him, strolling across the yard like nothing at all. I snap my attention back to Mom and try to control my face. I have to keep her distracted.

"Hey." I make it up as I go. "I—I, um. Did they say anything about what I missed at school?"

"The secretary said everything would be explained in the packet." She starts to turn.

"W-wait. Mom. What if I, uh." I flip through the pages without really looking at them. "What if I have questions?" Finally, he's out of view. "On second thought, never mind. Looks like everything is here. Thanks."

"You're welcome." She gives me a confused smile, then walks back toward the kitchen. "Oh, I got you peppermint candies, too, for your stomach."

That was too close.

When my heart stops racing, I take a closer look at the homework packet. Warren scrawled a riddle across the top of the page of math problems:

> If Eevee in another universe sneezes, and Eevee
> in this universe doesn't know she exists, does the
> sneeze make a sound?

Oh, that wacky Warren.

I turn the page and see a second note, also in his chicken scratch:

> Weirdness to share. Come by later if you're not
> contagious.

Weirdness? I flip through the rest of the pages, looking for clues, but there are only equations. From the kitchen, Mom blabs about her day. The Carsons stood her up for the open house way over in Mirabel, so her day was wasted driving back and forth to Scottsdale, and she really wants to land that deal, but they must be the flakiest people that ever walked the face of the earth and blah-blah-blah.

I turn back to Warren's second note. Danny weirdness, or something else? "I'm going to run out for a sec."

She pops her head around the kitchen doorway. "What for?"

"I have to ask Warren about some of this work."

"You can ask him tomorrow. He doesn't want your germs." She snaps the metal tongs in her hand. "I'm thinking stir-fry. Good?"

"Sure." When she's back in the kitchen, I flop back on the couch and cover my face with my arms. What am I doing?

I ditched school.

I lied.

I ditched school *again.*

I let him in my room. No one goes in my room. Not even my parents.

He kissed me.

I replay the scene in slow-mo in my mind.

It was a quick kiss. An unexpected kiss. But it was a kiss nonetheless.

"Someone's feeling better."

I gasp.

Mom's standing over me, holding a glossy magazine in her oven-mitt-covered hands. "Didn't mean to startle you. I thought reading something might help distract you from feeling bad. What were you smiling about?"

"Smiling?" I shrug. "Didn't realize I . . ." One of the article titles catches my eye: *Is It Love? How to Know for Sure!* "On second thought, reading sounds good."

She hands me the magazine. "Dinner will be ready in about ten minutes."

Just enough time to do a little research.

After dinner, I finish up the homework packet, then ping Warren on chat, but he's not online. I don't have any choice but to sit in the living room with Mom, watching stupid shows on TV. The whole time I think about Danny—one of the signs, according to the article. What is he doing? Is he thinking about me? What if he's thinking about the other me? Maybe I should call him. Am I overthinking this?

When the news comes on, Mom goes to bed grumbling

about having to work on a Saturday. I lock up the house and grab the peppermint candies. In my room, I stand in the place where he stood and stare at the walls. My brain is so wound up, there's no way I'm going to be able to sleep. I pull the paints out from under my bed.

Tonight the terdragon-curve fractal calms me. I close my eyes and let the design expand and fill my mind. The lines lengthen and snake around, each ending in a finlike curve. When I open my eyes, I break out my acrylics and set about painting the fractal across the border of the window. My hands work quickly, the imaginary equations mapping out the lines faster than my brush can follow.

Three taps at the window startle me out of my trance. Did I imagine them? I hold my breath and wait. When the sound comes again—*tap tap tap*—I peek through the slats and see him, backlit by the streetlight. I slide the window open.

"Saw your light," he whispers. "Thought I'd say hi."

"Hi."

"Wanna hang?"

Do I? "I'll be out in a sec."

I breathe down the butterflies in my stomach—also a sign from the article—pull a sweatshirt on over my pajamas, step into my sneakers and tiptoe down the hall.

The night is chilly and the air tastes fresh. It must be late. Dad's lights are off. Warren isn't on his roof. Danny sits in the grass, resting back on his hands with his legs crossed in front of him. I sit beside him.

The darkness feels so big, I keep my voice low. "What's up?"

"Today was almost perfect. I don't want it to end."

"Just almost perfect?"

"Just almost." He leans back on his elbows. "Things go okay after I left?"

"Almost."

"Just almost?"

"It's better now."

He points up at the sky. "There's the Big Dipper." He tracks his finger toward the horizon. "Which makes that Polaris."

"You know your stars."

"My dad taught me. The ocean's big. Read the stars and you never get lost."

"You must spend a lot of time at the ocean. Do you go over to California a lot?"

"Been a couple of times. It's a two-day sail, though. Mom worries when we're on the water overnight."

"Sail?"

"Well, we could fly, but then you don't see the stars." He brushes the grass off his hands. "So, what do you want to do tomorrow?"

"Hang on. Say that bit again about California."

"What?"

My head feels woozy. "Your Arizona has an ocean?"

"Yours doesn't?"

"Oh my God." I stand up and pace.

He stands, too, takes me by the hands, and leads me back to sit again on the grass.

"Was it an earthquake? Did part of California sink into the ocean?"

He makes a face like I'm crazy. "No. It's just always been

out there. Across the sound. So, tomorrow. What should we do?"

I pick a blade of grass, still trying to imagine Arizona Bay. The grass is smooth against my fingers. "Something legal?"

"Boring."

I pick a second blade and twist the two together. "Aren't you afraid of getting caught?"

"That's what makes it exciting."

"You and I are so different."

"That's what makes it exciting." He hooks his elbows around his knees and we just sit there, looking at each other. The streetlight illuminates half of his face, the bridge of his nose, the curve of his jaw. Finally, he breaks the silence. "Did you find it?"

"Find what?"

"That'd be a no, then."

"What did you do?"

He smirks. "You'll know it when you see it."

"Tell me."

"Nope."

"Please."

He looks up at the sky.

"Give me a hint."

He looks back at me and leans close. My heart flutters up in my throat and I swear the stars start to spin. "No," he whispers. And then he kisses me for the second time.

Really kisses me.

26

Danny

She tastes like peppermint.

I lie back in the grass and there are a bazillion diamonds above us. She lies down next to me, shoulder to shoulder. I want to kiss her again, but instead I find her hand and hold it in mine.

"*Now* it's perfect."

In the distance, a dog barks and there's the sound of a car engine. Eevee's fingers are tight around mine and I stroke the top of her thumb.

The night sounds fade to white noise. Then a steady pounding, at first in time with my heart but then separating into its own rhythm. Thick and constant, the beat slams against me. Courses inside. Above the droning, I hear voices I can't identify. Jumbled. Inseparable. Lights dance behind my eyes. Somehow, I'm no longer on the lawn at Eevee's house. Bodies slide against me, around me, pressing like ocean waves and always in time with the sound. A woman's laugh shudders through me and then her voice is in my ear. It's Eevee, only not. Every word lights up the colors in my eyes, bringing the world into focus. Strobe lights flash against bodies dancing, and before me her red lips, her slender arms around my neck.

"Danny."

The ground rushes up to meet me and I land. Hard. I gasp. Choke. She's leaning over me, her hands on my shoulders.

"Eevee?"

I touch the grass. Reach up and touch her face.

What was that?

She helps me sit up, then holds both of my hands in hers. "You must have drifted off and had a nightmare."

Pinpricks of cold race up my arms and circle my chest.

I don't think that was a dream.

27

EEVEE

Warren sets up the tubing while I dish out the custard powder. The chemistry lab whirs away with all fourteen ventilation hoods running, which is good. Missy's lab station isn't far from ours and we can't risk her listening in.

"Indicators definitely point to an EMP detonation," he says.

"And others on the underground agree?"

"Dark Web, Solomon." He tightens the lid on the jar. "The Underground is the subway system in London."

"Whatever. They agree?"

"They not only agree, they're spinning theories left and right. Some think he's Edgar Cayce returned. Others, that he's escaped from a mental hospital. The Dark Web's all abuzz with ideas about the parallel boy."

Mac holds up his hands (the universal teacher signal for *Your attention, please*) and the noise level in the room drops. If there's one teacher at Palo Brea who gets respect, it's Mac.

"Everyone, please be sure your venting hoods are turned on. Robert and Logan here just turned theirs off and nearly caused the school a code violation. When all stations are ready, we'll start the show."

The noise level rises again. I clamp the funnel to the stand. Warren pours in the custard powder. "Most of the theories are ridiculous, of course. One guy suggested he was the time traveler in that Charlie Chaplin film."

"Are you serious?"

"He even posted the video so I could decide whether or not the traveler looked like Danny."

"Did it?"

"Sure. If at some point Danny gains about two hundred pounds and starts wearing dresses."

"And you listen to these people?"

"Some of them." He attaches the hose to the Bunsen burner. "Oh, and I talked to Jordan. He made us an appointment for Monday afternoon."

I groan. "Now I just have to tell Danny."

"You haven't told him?"

"That we're going to turn him into a pincushion? Sorry, I haven't really found the right moment yet."

"We're not turning him into a pincushion." Warren checks the burner's setting. "It's just a routine physical assessment at a community-college health fair. No big."

I scratch the sparker across the burner but the flame doesn't ignite. "You're not the one on the examination table." Warren shrugs. "What else is out there on your Dark Web?"

"Some think he's an escapee from a secret government experiment, especially with all his talk about resistance." Warren tries the sparker, too, then rechecks the burner, hose, knob.

"That's creepy."

"I know, but there's no harm in looking at it from all angles." He puts the burner back on the table and makes a grumpy face. "We must have missed something."

"Like what? Clearly, it's not the same world we're in now."

"No, I mean with the burner."

I walk through the setup again. Everything looks right.

"How's it going?" Warren asks.

"Well, I don't see what we've done wrong here." I crouch to check the lines running under the table.

"I mean with him."

"Oh." My tongue trips me up and all I can get out is a squeaky "Fine." I stand again. "This should work. Is anyone else having problems?" I look around the room. The other tables are set up and ready.

Warren pulls the gas line from the burner and reattaches it. "We definitely need to talk to Mac."

"Okay." I turn to walk over to him, but Warren pulls me back.

"What are you doing?"

"Going to talk to Mac."

"Not *now*."

"But you said . . ." I point at the defective burner.

"I meant talk to him about the *situation*."

Mac appears on the other side of our lab table. "What situation?"

"Can't get the burner to light," I say.

Mac fiddles with the parts, the lines and knobs. He crouches under the table and bangs on the pipes, then picks up the clicker and scratches it. *Poof.* A perfect flame. "Voilà. Now, what situation? The fact that you two want to attempt something completely dangerous and illegal for the science fair?"

I glare at Warren. "What did you do?"

"Turned in our application." He ducks as if I'm going to hit him, and then looks confused when I don't.

"How about we talk after class." Mac knocks twice on our table and walks to the back of the room. "Stations ready? Safety goggles on? Fire shields up?" He holds his hand on the light switch, waiting for the go-ahead from the class. "As always, please remember this is a controlled experiment that should only be conducted in a safe environment with proper supervision. Now, drumroll, please."

The room goes dark and Mac begins the countdown. "Three. Two . . ."

On one, twenty-eight students behind safety shields release custard powder into fourteen Bunsen-burner flames. Fourteen spectacular flashes of fire light up the darkened room. I jump back. Missy screams. It's by far one of the coolest experiments we've done. We don't usually get to blow things up.

"It isn't the custard powder that ignites, but rather the corn flour in the mix. When the dust cloud disperses and mixes with the ample oxygen supply, you get flash combustion. Sometimes it isn't the obvious factor that causes the reaction."

Mac switches the lights back on. "You can turn off the vents. Be sure to follow proper cleanup procedures."

Warren and I break down our station, putting the different parts away in the storage cabinets.

"I can't believe you turned in that application," I whisper, pulling the tube from the Bunsen burner.

"And I can't believe you're having a problem with this. We're going to tell him anyway." Warren carries the funnel and tubing. We take our time, hanging around, waiting for everyone to finish cleaning up and clearing out.

Missy hangs around, too. I pretend to search through my chemistry book for some piece of important information so I can stay within earshot.

"What's it like, knowing you'll probably win the science fair this year?" She holds her hands behind her back and bats her blue eyes at Warren.

He clears his throat. "I. Well. You never know. We might not win." I look up, surprised. And not just because he thinks we might lose. Until recently, Warren could hardly form a complete thought in her presence. Why the change?

"Of course you will." She reaches out to smooth his collar. "You're so smart." Then her face changes to surprise. "I know. Maybe you could help me figure out my project for the fair."

Warren's mouth opens and shuts. I want to snap, *She can do her own work!*, but instead I bite my tongue and turn another page in the chem text. Mac finishes talking to a student and walks over to his desk. Now's our chance. I close the book loud enough to get Warren's attention, then nod at Mac. Warren swallows hard. "Um. Yeah. Maybe. Um. I gotta go, Missy."

"Oh." She picks up her books. "Well, let me know, okay?"

She smiles and turns to leave, her braids snapping like whips behind her.

When she's gone, I whisper, "Ready?"

Warren looks up, his face still red from blushing. "Let's do this." We walk together to the back of the room, where Mac is sorting papers at his desk.

"So . . ." Mac's glasses are perched up on his forehead. "The effects of EMPs on biological life forms. What sparked that idea?"

I start to answer, but two men in suits walk into the classroom. "Marcus McAllister?"

Mac frowns. "Yes?"

One of the men reaches into his coat and pulls out an ID. Just like in the movies. "We'd like a minute of your time."

Mac sets his hand on my shoulder and lowers his voice. "We'll continue this conversation later, but for now, the answer is no."

"No?" Warren sounds dumbfounded.

"Too risky. Find something else." Mac clears his throat and begins walking toward the suits. "What can I do for you?"

"Can we come by this weekend?" Warren asks.

Mac turns back and shakes his head. "Not a good time," he says.

No *and* not this weekend? Dejected and troubled, we grab our bags and shuffle from the room.

"Who were those guys?" I whisper as soon as the door shuts behind us.

"I don't know, but I wonder if it has something to do with Principal Murray hounding him on Friday. When you were out sick. Did you see the note I wrote on your homework?"

The weirdness.

"What happened?"

"He stood at the back of the room with his arms crossed, glaring at Mac the entire class period. I waited around as long as I could. As soon as the door shut, I heard Murray lay into him."

We wind our way through the crowds of students. I keep my voice low. "Do you think he's in some kind of trouble?"

"I hope not."

"Me too."

28

Danny

I suggested we do something interesting today, like take the bike out again and explore the part of town where the harbor should be. But instead, I navigated another day at Palo Brea, pretending to be someone I'm not. Got lost on the way to Spanish class. Fought to keep my eyes open through history.

Awesome.

But soon it will be over. Eevee will walk out of her last class and we'll be free to have fun again. Well, other than homework. But around Eevee, even homework isn't so bad.

I lean back against the soda machine—our designated meeting place—and close my eyes. What was up with that weird nondream last night? I saw my Phoenix. Even though it was a crazy mess, I knew that's where I was. I could feel it.

I think all the time about getting back there, but for the first time since I got here, it actually seems possible. Like I have a real shot. That I'll see my parents and Germ again. Maybe even Red Dress Eevee.

The last bell rings. Students spill out of classrooms onto the sidewalks, a wave of sound crashing the quiet. Not long to go now.

The weird thing is, what I felt first when I landed back on Eevee's lawn was relief. I should have been grasping to hang on to what I'd seen. What I'd lost. But all I could think about was Eevee in her ratty tennis shoes and how happy I was to be next to her.

The girl from the library, the one with the braids, walks toward me. I step to the side so she can get a soda, but she steps to the side, too. She doesn't want a drink. She wants me.

She shifts her books and sticks out her hand. "Hi, my name is Missy. I don't believe we've been introduced." So formal.

"I'm Danny."

"Pleased to meet you, Danny." She hugs her books in front of her. "You've been spending a lot of time with Warren and Eve."

Eve? I thought only Sid called her that. "I have."

"What are you guys working on?"

Who is this girl and why does she want to know? And what can I possibly tell her? Funny you should ask, Missy. I'm from a universe far, far away, and we're trying to figure out how to get me back there. It's super secret, though, so you can't tell anyone.

I clear my throat. "Nothing."

"Oh." She twirls one of her braids around her finger and looks at me like she's trying to read my mind. Or make up her own. She opens the cover of one of her textbooks and pulls out a folded paper. "Will you give this to Warren for me, please?"

"Sure." I turn the note over in my hands. It's fancy-folded into an octagon.

She gives me a stern look. "Don't read it." Then she turns and walks away.

Read it? I don't think I can even figure out how to open it.

29

EEVEE

Saturday morning Mom proposes we do something together, enjoy some mother-daughter quality time.

"Let's go to the mall." She sits on the edge of my bed, still in her bathrobe, her hair in a ponytail. "Or see that new movie with what's-his-name." She snaps her fingers to jog her memory. "You know. The one about the guy with the thing and the girl who helps him figure it out."

Sounds like my life.

"I can't today, Mom. Warren and I are working on our project for the science fair." Her face falls and I feel bad. "But we can go see what's-his-name when the project is done, if you want." This helps. Her face brightens and I'm free to get on with my day, helping the guy with the thing.

We take turns pushing the cart through O'Malley's Hardware, passing the lightbulb aisle, window treatments and plumbing.

Despite Mac's initial reluctance, we're moving ahead with our plan to build an EMP device. After all, we didn't even get a chance to argue our case before the suits showed up. Warren and I decided we'll either convince Mac of the necessity, or impress him with our creation. Besides, what other choice do we have?

Danny stops the cart. "Hop in."

I'm not the most graceful girl in the world, but I manage to crawl up into it without falling on my face or scraping my knees. Danny pushes off, his shoes squeaking against the polished concrete floors. I squeal as we career toward the paint section, narrowly dodging a forklift.

Danny slides to a sudden stop. I press my feet against the cart to keep from slamming into the metal basket. Warren jogs up as Danny picks a bunch of color sample cards from the paint display. Purples, magentas, greens. He tucks them into his back pocket and notices us watching him. "What? I like those colors." And we're off again, racing toward lumber.

Even with Warren's diagrams and shopping list, it takes forever to locate the right kind of wood, the right sizes. I wander around the lighting section while the guys watch an employee cut two-by-fours to the lengths we need. I like looking at the chandeliers. They make me think of stars. Finally, Warren and Danny come wheeling down the aisle, the cart full of supplies.

We pay for everything with Warren's freelance game-scripting fees and my birthday stash. Then we push the cart and carry our bags out to where Mrs. Fletcher is waiting with the minivan windows down and classical music playing. She has the patience of a saint. Of course it helps that Warren has convinced her we're gathering materials to conduct a groundbreaking experiment that will virtually guarantee his acceptance to MIT. Which might not be altogether untrue. We load the goods into the back, maneuvering the lumber through the seats all the way to the front.

When we get to Warren's, we reverse the process, unloading and carrying everything to the garage. Lucky for us, his parents are used to him doing wacky, large-scale experiments at home. Trebuchet, Jacob's ladder, replica TARDIS. They're so used to it, they've cleaned out half of the garage as his workspace and built a second shed in back to house his creations. They deserve some kind of award for being the coolest parents ever.

"Is that everything?" Mrs. Fletcher asks, her hands on her hips.

"Looks like it," I say, surveying the pile of stuff we've amassed. Warren nods.

"Good luck." She disappears into the house.

Coolest parents *ever*.

Warren looks at his watch. "Only have a couple of hours, but maybe we can get the framing done."

"You have plans?"

He looks away, then jumps in to help Danny sort the two-by-fours. "I'm going out."

"Out?" I cut the plastic wrapping from the rolls of chicken wire. "Out, like, to Arkham's Attic for comics?"

"No. Out, as in out."

"You mean a *date*?" I notice now that he's got his aviators on again, and he's wearing his favorite shirt—a ringer tee with a cartoon of Tesla on the front.

His answer is quiet. "Maybe."

I don't have to see his face to know he's blushing. "With Missy?"

That sets him off. He crosses his arms. "Yes, okay? I have a date with Missy. Is that such a big deal? Sheesh. It's not like it's the first time we've gone out."

"What?" I can't believe what I'm hearing. When did this start? How have I not noticed?

"Correct me if I'm wrong," he says, his voice acerbic, "but I don't have to get your permission to have a social life, Solomon."

From the look on his face, I can tell I've stepped way out of line. "I'm sorry," I say with as much sincerity as possible. "Of course you don't need my permission. I hope you two have a nice time."

But I can't help thinking about how she's been hanging around us. How yesterday she asked Danny about our science project. Warren wouldn't tell her, would he?

That night we walk circles around the neighborhood, listening to the cicadas sing and talking about nothing in particular. An orange half-moon hangs low on the horizon. Danny squeezes my hand. "Who else do you hope you are in your parallel worlds?"

The question throws me. I hadn't thought about it before, but he's obviously been thinking about it for a while.

How many versions of me are there out there? Theoretically, there could be an infinite number. Is it possible there's one for every dream I've had in my life here as myself? When I was a kid, I wanted to be a dancer, a teacher, an opera singer, an astronaut.

I think of her. The one other Eevee I *do* know about. Sometimes I want to be her.

It's taking me way too long to answer, so I choose the last thing I remember wanting to be before I fell in love with physics. "An archeologist." I kick a rock down the sidewalk. It rolls into a neighbor's yard. "Digging around ruins in Ireland or Rome. You?"

"Curator. At the Louvre."

"You have a Louvre, too?"

"We do."

I sigh. "I'd like to see the Louvre someday."

"Maybe you already have. Just not *you* you."

Warren sits on his garage floor, securing the last beam to the frame of the Faraday cage. It's bigger than I thought it would be—eight feet tall, at least—but I guess it has to be big enough for both Danny and the EMP device.

I keep wondering how his date with Missy went last night, but I don't dare ask. Instead, Danny and I staple chicken wire to the two-by-fours. I flinch every time I squeeze the grip of the industrial staple gun. *Bang.* I'm sure I look stupid, but I can't help it. *Bang.* I just—*bang*—always brace myself for the—*bang.*

Danny scoots the ladder over, climbs up and staples the wire to the top of the frame. *Bang. Bang.* I still flinch, but not as badly.

Warren steps back and inspects the work, pushing his goggles up on his forehead. "Looks good."

I've only ever seen pictures of Faraday cages, so I don't actually have any idea if he's right.

"It's not the first time I've made one, you know," he says.

Of course it isn't.

"I made a smaller one for the CAVE to keep my vintage computer collection."

Of course he did. *Bang.* Danny climbs down the ladder and starts working on another section. One quarter of one side of the cage is covered in chicken wire, and we still have a long way to go.

"Once we get it all set up, we'll wrap it in foil, too," Warren says. "Just to be sure."

I follow him over to the tool bench, taking off my work gloves. "If it's wrapped up, how will we see what's happening inside?"

"We won't, until we open the door." He takes a drink from a water bottle. "Or we just leave it closed and it'll really be like Schrödinger's Cat." He laughs. I smack him across the arm with my glove. "Geez, Solomon." He rubs the spot. "Lighten up. I'm kidding."

"Not. Funny."

He's in a good mood. I'm dying to know how the date with Missy went. Guess there's only one way to find out.

I keep my voice low. "How was the date?"

He fiddles with the water bottle cap. "Fine."

"Just fine? What did you guys do?"

"I don't know. Stuff. Talked." He turns to set the bottle on the workbench.

"Yeah? What did you talk about?"

"What is this, the Klingon Inquisition?"

"No, I'm just . . ." He didn't tell her, did he? About Danny? "Just curious. Sounds like you had a good time."

"I think we did." He smiles, but offers no further information.

"Cool." I fold up the fingers of the glove still in my hands and then let them flop back open. Talk about awkward. I shouldn't have asked.

"Did you tell him about tomorrow?" Warren whispers, eyeing Danny. I shake my head. "What are you waiting for?" He makes quiet chicken noises.

Danny walks over to us at the table, and gives Warren a funny look. I could tell him about the health fair now. But instead, I pick the EMP plans up and flip through the pages of instructions and diagrams, holding them for Danny to see as well.

"We have to make sure the pulse is confined to the cage," Warren says, "so we don't fry my house. Or your house. Or the city."

I lean back against the table. "How big of a pulse are we talking?"

"Well, that's the question, isn't it? How big is too big? How small is too small?" He walks over to the cage and pokes a finger through the chicken wire. His finger just fits. "We don't know the capacity of the pulse in Danny's explosion—"

"We don't even know if there was an EMP in that explosion. All of this is conjecture."

"Okay, but working from the hypothesis that there was one, we have to assume it was large enough to propel a guy his size from one universe to another."

I raise an eyebrow. "Assume?"

"Come on, Solomon." He frowns. "You're making this a lot more difficult than it needs to be."

"I just wish we had a better way to gauge this." What we need is guidance, expertise. I pull out my phone and dial. "I'm calling Mac."

Warren stops poking the cage. "He said this weekend wasn't a good time."

There's dead air for a beat, then the line connects and rings. And rings and rings and rings and . . . I hang up. "Seems like no time is good lately."

30

DANNY

"I can't believe you guys did that to me." I walk the bike in the gutter. Eevee and Warren share the sidewalk. He's trying to skate my board and I'm trying not to laugh.

"Oh, it wasn't so bad," Eevee says. "Just a couple of pokes."

"A couple? He must have stuck me twenty times."

They'd conspired, the two of them. Told me they had a great idea, a way to find out more about what might be going on with me. So after school, we rode-walked *three miles* only to end up at, what? A health fair. Twenty or so tables overflowing with pamphlets and diagrams. Diabetes awareness, nutrition information, cancer signs and symptoms. And at the last table, a dreadlocked vampire in latex gloves was waiting to take my blood. Some great idea.

"You could have warned me he was still learning."

Warren goes on the defensive. "Jordan's in his second year. He's almost finished his EMT training."

I look at the inside of my arm. The skin is already turning

purple where he jabbed me. With Warren, though, sometimes it's best to just smooth things over. "Hey, I'm just messing with you. I'm sure your friend will make a terrific doctor. Someday."

"EMT," Warren says, still annoyed.

"Well, I'm sure he'll make a terrific one of those, too."

A van drives by and I walk the bike up onto the sidewalk, out of the way.

"At least we know you're healthy," Eevee says. "This isn't because of some kind of . . ." She waves her hand around her head and shoulders. "Medical issue."

"Actually," Warren says, "we won't know that for sure until the blood results are in."

"And you haven't sent me to a shrink yet." I coast back down into the gutter, my feet lazy along either side of the bike. "Is that our next stop? Oh, wait, you're not going to tell me, right?" I look beyond her to Warren. "So, how are things going with Missy?"

Oops. Should've known better than to distract him. He trips and stumbles over the front of the board. Tries to stop himself from falling by taking huge steps, but it's hopeless. He crashes into the sidewalk with his shoulder and rolls.

"Warren!" Eevee crouches beside him, checks if he's okay. I fish the board out of a bush and reach over to help him up.

He takes my hand and makes a big show of brushing himself off. Then he looks past me. "Wait a sec." He lifts his goggles. "Didn't that van already pass us?"

Eevee and I look to where he's pointing. The white van approaches and drives by again. Can't see through the tinted windows.

"The driver probably just missed the house he was looking for the first time," I say. But they don't look so sure.

I pace the room, pain still gripping my chest as my thoughts spin off the hook.

It happened again. One minute I was lying on the bed, staring at the ceiling. Next thing I knew, static filled my head and I saw Germ. Hazy, like looking through a foggy window, but it was definitely him.

We were in a restaurant or something. Lots of noise, people talking and dishes clanking. "I don't see how we have a choice," he whispered. I tried to speak, but it was like talking underwater. My voice wedged in my throat. "I say we do it. Shake things up," he said. "Beat them at their own game."

I fought to push through to him, but something else pushed back. A wall-like force that grew stronger. Next thing I know I'm crashing to the floor next to my bed. An inch to the left and I'd have split my head open on the nightstand.

What's going on there, without me? What was Germ talking about? My gut tells me it has to do with Red December. But why would he be so stupid? We swore we were done with them. Unless things have turned so bad, Germ thinks the only option is to fight.

I need to get home. Even though going home will mean saying goodbye.

I flop back onto the bed, run my hands through my hair. Slide open the nightstand drawer and touch the cover of

Eevee's Vitruvian Man journal. Looks like he has a black eye, too.

I know almost nothing about the girl at the museum. Who I really want to know is the girl sleeping next door. I turn the book over in my hands. Maybe if I read it I could at least figure out *her*.

No.

It's 12:14. The last thing I want to do is get back in that bed and stare at the ceiling all night. I pull on a shirt and don't even bother with shoes. Slip through the house like a shadow and dash across the driveways.

I tap on her window, quietly at first, then louder. Her light goes on and the window opens. Just seeing her makes me feel better.

"Hey." Her voice is sleepy. "What's wrong?"

"I brought you something."

"Like a gift? At midnight?"

"Kinda."

She yawns.

"Sorry. I should have waited."

"No." Her smile is sleepy, too. "It's okay. Hang on."

The window slides shut and I don't have to wait long before she's at the front door.

"Here," I say, holding out the journal. "Take this. Please."

She turns the journal over in her hands and opens the cover. "My dad bought me this. He thought it would help with my writing."

"I keep taking it out of that drawer, thinking if I read your journal I'll learn more about you."

"Did you open it?"

I hold up my hands. "No. I swear."

"Well, you should have." She flips through the pages. "It's empty." She laughs and hands it back to me. "Keep it." Then she looks behind her, holds a finger to her lips and motions me in. I follow her through the living room and kitchen, our feet padding on the tile. She opens the back door really slowly, but the hinges still whine. We both freeze and listen, but there's just the hum of the fridge. I follow her outside, closing the door behind me with a quiet click.

The moon is low. The grass cold. Eevee looks like a ghost moving through the yard. She ducks beneath the branches of the mesquite at the far corner.

"Better than the front yard," she whispers. I set the journal down and we sit side by side, shoulders touching. Her hair has a clean, citrus smell. The branches block out most of the stars but the moon shines on our feet. Hers are small, almost dainty next to mine. She keeps her voice low. "You okay?"

"Sure."

She gives me a look.

"Okay, no." I rub my eyes with the heels of my hands. "It happened again."

"What did?"

"The nightmare thing. Except I don't think they're dreams."

She pulls her feet up and crosses her arms over her knees. "Maybe your mind is trying to process everything that's happened. That's what our brains do when we sleep."

"But I wasn't asleep. It just kind of hit me. Static and pulsing and then it's like I'm seeing somewhere else." I cross my arms on my knees, too, and look her in the eye. "Please tell me you believe me."

"You know I do."

She says that, but if I had to listen to this stuff, I'd think the person saying it was a nut job. "I saw Germ. There were a lot of people around and we were making some kind of plan."

Should I tell her about the work we did for Red December? Then what would she think of me? She'd probably never speak to me again. I wouldn't.

"It wasn't a memory?"

"No. This was new." I look across the yard, the moonlit grass and trees. "It was good to see him."

"I bet."

"Maybe next time it'll be my parents."

"Who was it the first time, when we were out front?"

My mouth opens and I'm looking at her, but I don't know what to say.

She's smart, though. Figures it out. "Ah." She nods and looks away. "Well, we're almost ready to build the EMP device. Then, hopefully, it'll work and you'll be on your way."

"Right."

"That's what you want, isn't it?"

"Yeah, of course."

"Then why do you sound sad?"

"I miss them, Eevee. I miss them so much. I keep thinking about all the little things. The way my mom hums when she does the dishes. The way she answers the phone. Dad's jokes, and how he chews his food." I rest my head on my arms and look at her. "It's weird what you remember about people when they're suddenly not around."

"Will you miss me?"

"Why do you think I'm sad?"

She fiddles with the fraying cuff of her sweatshirt. "But you'd have *her*."

"She's not you." I stretch my legs out in front of me and she does, too. We're silent for a moment, and then, "Do you want me to stay?"

Her answer is so quiet, if I weren't right next to her I wouldn't have heard it. She leans against me. I tip my head to the left until it rests on her shoulder. She tips hers to the right.

This is where I'd push the pause button if I could. Right here. The smell of her hair. The moon shining on our toes.

"I was thinking," she whispers, "it might be a good idea for you to check in with the foster family."

My head jerks up and I turn to face her. Talk about ruining a moment. "Why?"

"So Child Protective Services doesn't come looking for you."

Crap. I hadn't thought of that.

"Just make an appearance so they know you're not dead or lying in a gutter somewhere."

I hold out my arm in front of her. The angry circle-scars. "I could end up dead just being there." Her big eyes look into mine and I know she's right. "Okay, I'll do it."

"I wish there were another way."

"Me too."

She has no idea.

31

EEVEE

"Are you sure about this?" I look back to make sure Mrs. Fletcher is still parked at the curb. She's reading a book, clearly not concerned.

But I am. Probably because while I'm off on a treasure hunt with Warren, Danny is risking his neck at the foster home. I was an idiot suggesting he go there. Just like I'm an idiot for agreeing to come with Warren to some stranger's house on a Tuesday afternoon to get supplies for Project DELIVR.

We decided to give what we're doing a code name, in case anyone is snooping (like Missy, though Warren denies it). DELIVR stands for Device Engineered to Launch Inter-universal Visitation and Return. The Return part isn't really in the plan, but we needed something for the R. Warren lobbied for "DELIVERANCE" but there were just too many letters.

I'm glad Mrs. Fletcher is watching out for us. Warren told her it would take us ten minutes to make the trade, but she said if we're not out in fifteen max, she's coming in. Appar-

ently they argued a bit about the necessity of this trip. I guess despite being used to Warren's eccentricities, even she has her limits.

Warren walks up the short path to the fourth condo on the left, number 412. The door is blue. "Of course I'm sure. I've known Darwin's Dog for years."

"You met him online. You don't even know what his real name is."

"Well, it's time to find out." He rings the doorbell. A dog barks, but I can't tell if it's coming from inside or the condo next door. They're so close together. The curtains in the window of 412 move, the handle of the blue door turns, and I brace myself for . . . what am I expecting, anyway? An ax murderer? A drug-dealing Mafia kingpin? A spooky death clown? I take a step back, as if Warren's stick-figure body is going to protect me.

The door opens an inch before a chain stops it. The barking dog yaps its head off. The guy answering the door grumbles at it before peering through the inch gap. Sunlight glints off his sunglasses. Who wears sunglasses indoors? I'm ready to turn and run when he asks in a low voice, "What two things are infinite?"

"The universe and human stupidity," Warren answers. "And I'm not sure about the universe."

An Einstein quote as a password. Nice.

The door shuts and there's the sound of the chain being unlatched before the door opens again, wide enough to see the guy we've come to trade with. Except the person behind the sunglasses isn't a guy.

"Darwin's Dog?" Warren sounds surprised, too.

She stands just a little taller than me, wearing an Arizona State University T-shirt. Her black hair is pulled into a ponytail, her face serious. "Are you Mastermind?"

I snort and they both glare at me. "Sorry."

"Don't mind her," Warren says. "She's innocuous." He gives me a *Don't mess this up* look.

"Did you bring it?" Darwin's Dog asks. Warren nods and takes the backpack from his shoulder. "Not out here," she hisses, and she opens the door wider. I take one last look at Mrs. Fletcher, still reading her book, before following Warren inside. The clock is ticking.

I've never been in a college student's apartment, but this is what I kind of expected. Mismatched beanbag chairs. Milk crates for bookshelves. Scuffed-up coffee table strewn with empty plates and game controllers. The walls, though, are covered with really cool modern art. Stuff like Danny might paint.

Danny. A sizzle of panic races through me. He should be at the foster home by now. Is he safe?

Darwin's Dog walks to the kitchen, where sunlight streams through bay windows overlooking a patch of yellowed grass. On the table sits a sewing machine and neatly folded fabric. She slides the silver cloth across the table toward Warren. "I serged the seams and edges. Wasn't sure what you're using it for—*and I don't want to know*. All the same, I didn't want the seams coming apart on you."

"I appreciate that." Warren unfolds a section and looks at it closely. "Excellent." He sets his backpack on the floor and unzips the main pocket. A guy with serious bedhead walks into the kitchen from a door behind me and I gasp, startled. He nods at Darwin's Dog and goes to the fridge, pours himself a cup of orange juice and exits out another door. Warren, unfazed by the random visitor, pulls a manila envelope from his backpack and sets it on the table.

"Can I do the honors?" Darwin's Dog asks.

"Sure," Warren says. "It's yours now."

Suddenly I feel very third wheel. I don't have a fancy code name. I have nothing to trade. I'm just an accessory. Innocuous, as Mastermind said.

If I did have a secret code name, what would it be? EV, like Danny painted under the bridge? I like that, except it sounds just like my real name. Not much of a secret.

With delicate hands, Darwin's Dog opens the envelope flap and slides out the contents: cardboard. Then she lifts the top piece of cardboard and a smile consumes the part of her face not covered by the sunglasses. "Unbelievable," she whispers. She picks up the plastic-encased comic book for a closer look. "*Strange Tales,* number 110."

"First appearance of Doctor Strange," Warren says for my benefit. "Mint condition."

"Where did you find it?" she asks.

Warren's face hardens. "You don't name your sources. I don't name mine."

"Right," she says, remembering herself. "Of course."

"It's a trade, then?" Warren asks.

"Absolutely."

He picks up the fabric, folds it to fit in his backpack and closes the zipper. The *Star Wars* Cantina song fills the kitchen.

Darwin's Dog and I look at each other, confused. Warren pulls out his cell phone and looks at the screen. "Voyager One is ready for departure." He slings the backpack over his shoulder and extends his hand to Darwin's Dog. "Pleasure doing business with you."

She nods and walks us to the door. "See you online, Mastermind."

And like that, our mission is complete.

"How much was that comic book worth?" I ask Mastermind as we walk back to the car. I half expect to see a white van waiting for us. But there's only Mrs. Fletcher with the engine running and a pleasant look on her face.

"It was a fair trade."

"Really? Seems like the comic book would have been worth a lot more than fabric."

"Metallic weave can be very pricey, especially the kind made with copper." Warren shrugs. "Doesn't matter, though. I have an even better copy of *Strange Tales* 110 back home in the vault."

I stop and stare at this friend I've known for so many years. What other secrets does he have locked away?

32

Danny

There's a boy in the front yard poking the dirt with a stick. He looks up when I get closer. Smiles huge. Runs over and wraps his arms around my legs.

"Danny." He squeezes like mad.

"Hey, you." I muss his hair and try to remember if he was in the pictures hanging on the fridge.

"Why'd you go away?"

My heart caves. I crouch down and he wraps his arms around my neck. "Sorry, little man. I had some stuff to do."

"Work stuff?"

"Yeah." I hug him back. "Something like that." He's super skinny. I can feel his ribs.

He won't let go, so I stand up and we walk into the house like that, with him hanging around my neck, squealing.

The place stinks like onions and mildew. The screen door slams and a woman steps out of the kitchen, wiping her hands on a towel. She looks pissed. I lean down, but the little guy won't let go.

"Get off him, Ben."

Ben. I poke him in the armpits and he squirms away. Runs over and grabs a toy airplane and zooms it around.

"Where the hell have you been?" the woman asks. "What is it, Tuesday? Haven't seen you in more than a week."

"Had some stuff to figure out."

"Oh. Well, how nice for you." She sniffs and walks back to the kitchen. "Sam called. Fired you for not showing up. Way to go." She picks up a knife and pulverizes an onion.

"I'll, uh, go talk to him. See if I can get it back."

"Him?"

"Her?"

She stops chopping and glares at me. "Are you hanging out with that Neil again?"

Who? "No."

"Better not be." The knife pounds the cutting board. Ben orbits around. She points the blade at me. "If we find out you are . . ."

"I'm not. I swear." I hope I'm not lying.

She sniffs again. Scoops the onion into a pot and puts it on the stove. "Brent'll be home soon. Better make yourself invisible until dinner."

I walk down the hall toward Danny's room. One of the other doors is open. A girl with headphones sits cross-legged on a bed. She doesn't look up. I close Danny's door behind me.

Coming here was a bad idea. The bastard is going to show up and beat the snot out of me.

Right. No point in sticking around for the show.

I rifle through the dresser. May as well take what I can and get the hell out.

I'm looking under the bed when I hear the door open. Ben walks into the room, zooms the plane around, buzzing his lips for engines. I sit up on my knees. He sits on the bed. "Wanna play?"

"Sure, Ben."

He looks at me, his brows scrunched. "You call me Benny."

"I do? I mean, right. Benny." I make an airplane with my hand and fly it around. Crash it into the mattress and make explosion sounds. Benny cackles like it's the funniest thing he's ever seen. He crashes his plane into the bed and explodes spit all over the place. I think about Brent and my stomach clenches.

"Hey, Benny?"

His airplane is in the air again. Zoom. Zoom.

"Does Brent ever get mad at you?"

His eyebrows scrunch down for a split second. Then he crashes the plane and explodes it and laughs. Raises the plane up again.

"Benny? Does he ever—"

"I don't want to play." He hops off the bed and runs out the door.

I punch the bed, then the wall. I can't leave knowing my having been here will piss Brent off. There's no way. Better to stay and take the hits.

There's a phone on the nightstand. I dial Eevee's cell but her voice mail picks up. "Hey, Eevee. It's me." My voice sounds strange in my ears. "I'm going to stick around here for a bit. Through dinner at least. Just to make sure things are cool."

I set the phone down and think of what she'd said. About making things better for Danny. Maybe she's right. Maybe there's a way.

I find Benny in the backyard, already over our conversation. We run races. Blow bubbles and chase them around the dead grass. Swing on the rickety set. Ben laughs himself into hiccups.

The woman—I don't even know her name—drags a garbage can out the back door. I leave Benny on the swing set and run over to her. "Let me."

She looks shocked, but nods and goes back inside.

I empty the garbage into the dumpster in the alley and walk the can back to the kitchen. Whatever she's cooking covers the stink of the house. I peek inside the cabinets, not sure where to put the thing back.

"Here." She opens the door next to the sink and I slide it in place.

"Anything else I can help you with?"

She looks at me hard. "No," she says. And then, in a quieter voice, "Thank you."

"You're welcome."

When I find him in the sandbox, Benny's still hiccuping.

●

We're sitting around the table when Brent walks through the front door. He takes one look at me and laughs. Not a fun kind of laugh. A laugh that stops everyone at the table cold. Marta—the girl with the headphones—drops her fork. It clangs on the plate and everyone jumps.

"Sorry," she says under her breath.

Brent throws his hat on the counter and grabs a brew from the fridge. Sits at the table and cracks open the can. He never takes his eyes off me.

"How was work?" the woman asks. The kids—there are five of us—eat in silence.

"Don't want to talk about that. When did he show up?"

"After school," she says.

I scoop up the chili and pretend not to hear him. Deflect attention. Nothing to see here.

"Danny and me did bubbles," Ben says, but the woman shushes him and he pouts.

Brent takes another swig and wipes his mouth on the back of his hand. Belches. "Where you been?"

I chew to buy time. Remind myself this is for Danny's sake. Benny's, too. And Marta, and the twin boys with their white-blond hair and haunted faces. "At a friend's house."

"Which one?"

"I don't think you know her."

"Her?" He laughs and spit dribbles down his chin. He wipes it on his shoulder. "A girl?"

They all look at me. "Yes, sir."

He nudges the woman with the back of his hand. "Did you get that? *Sir.*" He raises the can to drain it. "Get me another one, Sooz."

Sooz goes to the kitchen and returns with another brew. Before she sits, she opens it for him.

"Got yourself a girlfriend, eh?" His stomach shakes as he laughs. "What would any girl see in a loser like you?"

I breathe in, breathe out.

"She must be a real basket case."

My hand goes tight around my spoon. I look at Ben. Focus on his fuzzy mop of curls. "Actually, she's really nice. Smart, too."

"Right." Brent scoops up his chili. A pig guzzling slop.

"She is." I take a sip of water. "One of the smartest girls at school."

"Don't take that tone with me."

Sheesh. "I'm sorry." I keep my voice as blank as I can.

"Yeah." He wipes his mouth again and sits back in his chair. "You are."

"May I please be excused?" Marta asks. Sooz nods and the girl slips away from the table without a sound.

"Can you do us all a favor, Danny?" Brent says. "Don't get this girl knocked up. We don't need any more little losers in the welfare line."

I imagine taking the spoon and scooping out his eyes. Really slow. But instead I take a bite of chili and look at Sooz. "This is really good."

She nods and gives me a confused look.

I want to tell her—tell both of them—that I know this game. That he's baiting me. Wants a fight. Wants it more than anything else.

But I'm not playing. Not tonight.

I scrape the bowl. It really is good chili. Eevee's probably having dinner with her mom right now. I wonder if she told Sid I wouldn't be there. I hope she got my message.

"May I please be excused?" I ask as politely as I can.

"No." Brent's laugh is like a rake up my back. "You can sit right where you are and tell us where you've really been."

"I told you."

"What's this girl's name?"

"Eve."

His laughter explodes and the boys flinch. "This gets better by the minute. Does she live in a garden?"

I sit on my hands so I don't wring his neck. "She lives on—" I stop myself. "Down off Thunderbird Road."

"You're telling the truth," Sooz says, like she can't believe it.

"I am."

But Brent won't let up. "Call her."

Really? I tighten my jaw to control my face. Force a smile. "Okay."

It takes me a minute to find the phone with all the crap cluttering the kitchen counter. I dial Eevee's number, hoping she doesn't pick up, but knowing if she doesn't, I'm toast. It rings. Rings. Rings.

And she answers.

I swallow. "Hi." Brent watches me with his eyes half-sunk in disgust. Or a beer fog. Can't tell which.

"Hey," Eevee says. "I got your message. Are you okay?"

"Yeah." I keep my voice low. "Just wanted to say hi."

"What's wrong?"

Brent gets up from his chair, hoisting up his pants. "I want to talk to this girl."

Unbelievable. "Um, Brent wants to talk to you."

"Who?"

He takes the phone from me before I can answer. Or warn her.

"Is this Eve?" He looks at me like he's caught me in a lie, and then his face drops. "Oh. Well." He winks at me. "Danny here tells me you've got the hots for him. Is that true?"

Breathe in. Breathe out. Keep cool.

"Aw, just friends. Sorry to hear that. He thinks you're a real piece. Says you're smart, too. Didn't know Danny liked the brainy type. Well, here's your Romeo. Nice talking to you. Don't bite any apples."

He hands the phone to me like he's won some kind of victory, then he smacks both hands on the table so the plates rattle. "Clean this up," he barks. Sooz and the twin boys jump out of their chairs and get to work.

Eevee yells in the receiver. "Danny?!"

I put the phone to my ear. "I'm here."

"I don't think you should stay there." She sounds panicky.

"I can't really leave yet," I say low, watching Brent. I'm sure he's still listening. Gathering ammunition.

"He scares me. Be careful."

"I will." I make my voice cheery. "I'll see you tomorrow at school, okay?"

"Leave as soon as you can."

"Okay," I say. "See you later."

I hang up the phone. Dodged that land mine. But how many more will Brent set? It's going to be a long night.

I take a stack of plates from Sooz and we walk into the kitchen. At the sink she whispers, "Is she nice?"

"Very." I smile, but all I can think is, just friends?

33

EEVEE

"Honey?"

How long have I been standing here listening to dead air? I put my cell phone down on the counter.

"Everything okay?" Mom pulls a pan from the oven and closes the door with a one-two of her knee and elbow.

Is he in danger? Should I go over there and help him? Why did that Brent guy want to talk to *me*? This is Danny we're talking about, though. If anyone's a survivor, it's him. "Everything's fine."

Mom dishes out lasagna onto two plates and hands them to me. "Anyway, the Carsons loved the house. They want to compare it with a couple others, but I think they're going to put in a bid. Isn't that great?"

It takes all my strength to sit through dinner. I eat my lasagna, pass the butter when asked, and listen to Mom talk about stuff I don't care about while my imagination runs wild with what might be happening to Danny. When we're finally finished and the dishes are clean, I head over to Warren's to work on the EMP device.

I find him high up on the ladder, attaching Darwin's Dog's fabric to the Faraday cage. Now, rather than a chicken coop, the thing looks like a contraption in a magician's set. A big box draped in shiny cloth with a little door, perfect for going in through and never coming back out.

"There you are, Solomon." Warren's words are muddled by the nails he's holding with his lips. "Wondered if you were coming."

"Sorry. Dinner took longer than I expected." I see Danny's work gloves on the table and swallow down my nerves. "Tell me what to do." Quickly, say anything to distract me.

Warren places the next nail and bangs the hammer, making me jump. "Instructions are on the worktable," he says, preparing to strike again. "You should review them."

I smooth the pages of the printout and read through the steps, identifying the parts Warren has arranged on the garage floor. Circuit board. Capacitor. Steel block. And more copper wire than I've ever seen in my life.

Warren sets the hammer and several unused finishing nails on the table. "Questions?"

Questions? Yeah, I've got questions. Like, what in the world have we gotten ourselves into here? "Directions are pretty straightforward."

"Okay. Let's get started."

Warren switches on the overhead lights and closes the garage door. Before it's all the way down, I take a quick look, hoping to see Danny walking toward my house. He isn't.

"Here." Warren hands me a spool of wire and the first two pages of the plans. "You do steps one through three. I'll go build the timer circuit."

I check the instructions again, just to be sure. I can't believe we're doing this.

"What'd you say?" Warren asks.

"I said, I can't believe we're doing this." I didn't realize I'd been thinking out loud.

"We'll keep it contained. Don't worry."

I lift up one end of the steel block and begin wrapping the wire around it to create the copper coil. The block is like a heavy shoebox. If I drop it, my fingers are toast. I pull the wire around it, trying to make the coil as tight as possible. Soon my index finger begins to sting where the wire rubs, even with the work gloves. "I was thinking," I say, taking off my glove and rubbing my finger, on which there's a painful red line. "After the test run, we should go see if Mac is home."

Warren doesn't look up from his work. "Good idea."

We continue on in silence for who knows how long. The coil done, I measure out the remaining wire. Three feet. Warren stands and brushes off the knees of his pants. He flips through the directions again. "Timer mechanism is done. Let's connect the coil."

We carry our halves of the device to meet in the middle, then connect them into one dangerous unit.

"You know what's scary about this?" I ask.

"What?"

"How easy it is."

We stand back and look at our work. Doesn't seem like much really—a bunch of wires, circuitry, and a simple switch to turn it on. Still, it should be enough to generate a substantial pulse.

"What if it doesn't work?" Warren asks.

I think about what Danny said last night, under the tree. About leaving. About me. "What if it does?"

"I guess we'll find out. Let's move it onto the platform and put it inside the cage." He scoots a wooden flat over to our workspace. We assemble the parts on top first, then carry the whole thing over to the cage. The door is narrow, and we have to tilt the platform to squeeze it through. Then we're standing inside with our terrible creation and I'm trying not to imagine Danny in here.

"Can we at least put a chair in here, so he's comfortable?"

"You can hang curtains for all I care, as long as it still works." He lifts up his goggles and gives a wicked grin. "Let's throw it out of the nest and see if it can fly."

I follow him out of the cage—it's darker in there now that it's covered with cloth—and the garage light glares in my eyes. Warren pulls a scientific calculator out of a toolbox and walks back into the cage. He emerges again empty-handed, and secures the cage door. "The timer's set. We'll know it worked if the calculator's circuits are fried."

We move to the far side of the garage. Warren holds up his stopwatch and we huddle to watch the seconds wind down.

"Is this how it will go tomorrow?" I'm not sure why I'm whispering.

"Yes."

Except tomorrow there'll be a person inside the shiny magician's box.

A person I care about.

Ten seconds. Five. And then three, two . . . The alarm on the stopwatch sounds. Warren clicks the button to turn it off.

"What, that's it?" I ask. "No explosion?"

Warren walks toward the cage. "Nope. EMPs are silent. If they're attached to an incendiary device, then there'd be a boom." He opens the door. "We didn't build a bomb, remember?"

Of course. Duh.

By the time I get through the door, he's already cheering, punching the buttons on the calculator.

He hands it to me. The screen is black. The circuits are dead.

"And . . ." He scoops up something from the platform. "Look." He unfolds his cupped hands. On his palm sits a tiny, and likely scared, gecko. It flicks its ringed tail, and Warren laughs as it scurries up his sleeve.

I cross my arms. "You know I said no animals."

He catches the lizard again and carries it out the side door. "We had to make sure it was safe."

I watch, relieved, as it darts off into the shadows.

●

It's dark by the time we reach Mac's street. One by one, the streetlights flicker on.

"What if we're going about this the wrong way? What if blasting Danny with an EMP makes it worse?"

Warren walks with his hands in the pockets of his khakis. "What if it makes him better? What if it's like allergy shots? You inject more of the irritant into the system and the body learns to fight it off."

"Or it causes shock and the person dies." I stretch my neck side to side. Too much tension.

A nighthawk swoops overhead, its white-striped wings illuminated by the nearest streetlight. The nights are getting warmer. Soon the temps will climb and spending any time outside, even at night, will be unbearable. Will Danny still be here then? I fold my arms over the knot in my stomach. We walk up Mac's gravel drive. The lights are off, but that doesn't always mean anything. Warren rings the doorbell and we wait.

"What's that sound?" I look toward the shop, the house behind Mac's, across the street. It's hard to tell which direction it's coming from.

"Sounds like lawnmowers." Warren knocks three times on the door.

"Who mows the lawn at night?"

We wait, but Mac doesn't answer. Warren walks toward the shop and I follow. The sound of the engines grows louder, but there's no sign of Mac. "Looks like we came here for nothing."

The lights are off in the shop, too. I cup my hands around my eyes and peer through a dark window. It isn't that the lights are off; the windows are blacked out. What in the world?

I knock and put my ear to the shop door while Warren walks around the far end of the building. Just a moment later, he's back, tugging on my sleeve. "Look what I found." I see his lips moving but can barely hear his voice.

"Something strange . . ." My voice trails off as I round the corner. The engine sound is so loud now, we both have to cover our ears. Tucked behind the bushes at the far side of the building, three generators rattle away. Thick power lines lead from the generators to a hole cut in the shop wall. In all our work with Mac, welding and stuff, we never had to use anything but the regular electricity. What could he be doing that would require that much juice?

We continue around the other side of the shop—it's a skinny space between the building and the fence—and walk the length back toward the sidewalk. The windows on this side are blacked out, too. When it isn't so loud anymore, I uncover my ears. "Do you think he's in there?"

"He probably can't hear us." Warren starts toward the sidewalk but I pull him back.

"Look." Across the street, a few houses down, sits a white van. The headlights are off, but the running lights glow yellow. We duck away from the corner. I press my back against the shop wall. "Tell me that isn't the same van."

Warren doesn't say anything at first. Then, "It probably isn't." But I can tell from his face that he thinks it is, too.

How long has it been there? Did it follow us? Surely we would have noticed, right?

"I don't think we should go back that way," I say. My legs feel numb.

"What would you suggest we do?"

"Go another way."

He rolls his eyes at my nonhelpful answer. Then he looks past me toward the high fence separating Mac's backyard from the others. "We could jump it."

"Are you crazy? We won't make it over." I shake my head. "If we do, we'll get busted by Mac's neighbors for trespassing."

He peeks around the corner of the building again. His shoulders relax, and he steps out into plain view. "It's gone."

"What?" I glance around the corner to see for myself. Leaves rattle across the street. The spot where the white van was sitting is empty.

●

We don't say much on the walk home, but both keep looking behind and around us. We decide it was probably nothing. Our concern for Mac had us in a state of heightened awareness and we made an illogical connection between two unrelated white vans, neither of which had ever posed any kind of threat. By the time we reach our own street, we're relaxed enough to laugh at how silly we behaved, and take turns mimicking each other's freaked-out expressions.

Warren hops up onto the lava rock. "Tomorrow is D-day, then?"

My stomach ties itself back into a knot. "Guess so."

"Cool. See you then, Solomon." He makes the Spock sign before hopping down and walking inside his house.

I spend what's left of the evening at my desk with my

textbooks, but instead of studying I watch out the window for Danny. He should have been back by now. When it gets late, I change into my pajamas and look out the window. Brush my teeth and look again. Then I lie on my bed and stare at the ceiling. For the first time in days, I don't hear his knock.

34

Danny

I hole myself up inside Danny's room and pace, waiting for the house to fall asleep. It's taking forever. I can still hear the television in the family room and voices down the hall.

Once I'm sure everyone's asleep, I'll slip out and race back to Eevee's. Tomorrow is EMP Day. If all works out like it should, I go home. Which means I'm dinking away my last hours in this hellhole instead of with her. Argh.

I check the time—10:07—and flop onto the bed. Death-metal posters stare down at me. I lie there and lie there and listen and wait.

My chest tightens and my eyes blur. Waves pulse through me as monotone whispers bubble up through the static.

I feel safe and secure. No one wants to harm me.

Compliance is good. I relinquish control.

I feel safe and secure. No one wants . . .

Through the haze, I see a white dome splashed with pulsing blue lights. The voices swarm, overlapping, weaving in and out. I feel nothing. Detached. Weightless.

A woman's scream pierces through and I'm jerked back from the edge. My arms clutch at the mattress, the pillow, anything solid. Death metal stares me in the face. I roll over and the room keeps going. Put my feet on the floor and fall. Knees hit the carpet. I hold my head to keep it from spinning apart.

And then I hear him.

Brent.

I crawl toward the door. Crumbs and dirt cling to my palms. This place is a hole. I rest against the jamb and reach up to turn the handle. The door swings open an inch and their voices burst in.

"Where's it all going, Brent?"

"Who the hell do you think you are, talking to me like that?"

"We need money."

"It was your idea to take in all of these leeches. That's what they are. Leeches. Sucking us dry."

"Those *kids* keep food on the table."

There's a sharp sound and I'm on my feet, praying he hit the counter, the wall, anything but her. As I inch down the hallway, though, I hear her crying. My hands sliding along the wall curl into fists.

When I get to the end of the hall, I see him there in the kitchen, arms crossed. The fluorescent light glares down. I lean forward and see the top of Sooz's head by the cabinets. Crying in her hands. She grips the counter, pulls herself up. Holds one hand to her face.

"This is my house, dammit." Brent points his finger. "I

won't be talked to like that in *my house*." He pokes her twice in the chest.

Her hand falls to her side. She speaks slowly, her voice low. "What are you spending the money on this time?"

He raises his hand and my pulse hammers in my head. The walls go tunnel vision. I step into the open and her eyes flick to me. He turns his head.

"This ain't your business, Danny."

She gives me a look that says *Run*. But I won't. Not this time. I step into the room and lock my eyes on Brent, his hand still raised. She shakes her head at me but I don't move. With everything I have, I stare him down. Make sure he knows.

I see him. All he is and all he'll never be, I see.

He covers his initial flinch with a sneer, but we both know he's weak. He lowers his hand and mutters, "Don't need this crap." Grabs his keys and slams the door behind him.

Sooz steadies herself on the counter and covers her mouth. Exhales hard. Goes to the fridge.

"Let me," I say. The freezer air bites my hot face. I pull out a bag of peas, wrap them in a towel and hand them to her.

Her eyes are hard, but she nods and holds the cold up to her cheek. Winces when the towel makes contact.

"Why do you put up—"

She holds up her hand. Shakes her head. Her lip is swelling. "Go. You're better off away from here."

"What about when he comes back? What about them?" I point toward the hall, where I hope the others are still sleeping.

"He won't hurt them. But you . . ." She takes the towel

down, licks her lip. "It's better if you stay with your friend. At least for now."

I don't know if I've just helped things or screwed them up. "I'm afraid . . ."

She laughs. "No you're not. You've never been afraid. Not that I've seen, anyway." She fixes the towel where it's unwound from the peas and touches the cold back to her face. "Go on. I'll keep things together."

When she sees I'm not moving, she insists. "Go."

My feet carry me down the hall. I'm like a deflated balloon, floating. I grab my wallet and pull on my shoes.

Back in the kitchen, she sits at the counter with the phone in her hands. I stop at the doorway.

"Check in with me?" she asks. "Let me know you're okay?"

"Here." I grab a pencil from a jar near the sink and write down Eevee's number. My voice catches. "Give Benny a hug for me."

"I will."

I pick up my things and head for the door. Before I go, she says, "Danny?" Her swollen lip distorts her smile. "Thank you."

I nod and close the door behind me, feeling like half my heart is still there, inside.

Outside, it's that murky time of morning when it feels like the sun will never rise. The world around me is quiet. Just the sound of my shoes on the sidewalk.

The lights of a corner gas station catch my eye, give me an idea. Maybe there's another way to help. On the far side, I find the pay phone. The receiver is cold against my ear. I press zero, and when an operator answers, I whisper-croak, "I need to report some kids being abused." She's silent a second before saying "One moment" and the line clicks and rings again.

"Phoenix Police, what's your emergency?"

"There's a man named Brent abusing kids at a foster house." I give her the address and hear her dispatch a car.

"How are you aware of this situation?" she asks.

"I'm one of the kids."

"What is your location?"

I hang up the phone. They have all the information they need. Hopefully, they'll go and see and help. I close my eyes and think of Benny, asleep in his bed.

Please let it help.

I try to shake the tired from my arms. This body feels worn out, but I gotta keep moving. Hands tucked into my pockets, I carry on toward Eevee's, the night's events again replaying in my head. Brent's gravelly voice. Sooz's cries.

My feet stop.

A white dome with flashing lights. A cloud of voices surging through the void.

"Oh no." I run a hand over my face as adrenaline jolts me awake. "Shit." My feet start moving again. Fast. Please don't let it be what I think. Please don't let it be what I . . .

I'm dragging by the time I reach Eevee's street. The moon has long set and the stars are beginning to fade. Even though my legs are screaming, I break into a jog. I can't get to her fast enough.

35

EEVEE

As soon as I hear the tap on my window, I run to the front yard. One look at his face and I know whatever he went through, it was awful. "Did he hurt you?"

He shakes his head.

"I'm sorry. It was a stupid idea. You should've said no."

He holds my face in his hands. His lips feel dry against my forehead. With a groan, he falls into a heap on the front step and exhales. "It was the right thing to do."

"I was so worried." My knees go weak, so I sit beside him before I fall. It's dark out and there's a chill in the air. The cold concrete makes me shiver.

"I'm in trouble, Eevee." He rubs his face. "Big trouble."

"With Brent?"

"No." He raises his face to the sky and closes his eyes. "Back in my world."

"It happened again?"

He nods.

"What was it this time?" I'm scared to ask, but I can't *not* know.

He rests his forehead on one hand, his elbow on his knee and his eyes still closed. The muscle on his jaw flexes tight. "There's this program they use for compliance offenders. I don't know anyone who's been through it, but you hear stories about it. It's got some fancy name, but on the street everyone calls it Hydro. First they break you with deprivation and then they reprogram your thinking." He looks at me and sighs. "I'm pretty sure what I saw was the inside of a Hydro tank."

"Which means . . ."

"Danny got caught breaking the law."

"Wow." I can't believe what I'm hearing. "It's like something from a Bradbury novel."

"The thing is, they wouldn't put him in there for a first offense. Not unless it was something huge."

My brain feels like it's two steps behind. Slowly the pieces begin to click into place. "Wait. What are you saying?"

He tucks his hands behind his knees. "I think they're punishing him for something I did. Before I got here. If I go back, I'm done. If I don't go back, Danny takes the blame."

"For what? What did you do?"

He doesn't answer. He just stares at the grass. Putting his own puzzle pieces together, I'm sure.

We spend what's left of the night on the porch swing, sitting in silence, waiting for the sun to rise.

"Where is he?" Warren looks at his watch for the fourteenth time.

"Would you chill out?" I don't even try to hide the annoyance in my voice. "He said he'd only be a minute."

"That was..." He checks his watch again. "Six minutes ago."

Warren's wound up tighter than the copper coil. We're behind schedule. If we don't set the EMP off soon, *he'll* explode. I'm about to remind him he's a scientist and shouldn't be so easily ruled by his emotions when the garage door opens. My stomach twists and I can't quite breathe. I guess I should remind myself the same thing.

Danny walks in, holding something in his hands. "Hey."

"What took you so—"

"He's here," I say, holding a hand up to Warren. "Okay? Breathe."

Warren disappears into the cage, muttering I'm the one who should breathe. He's right. I exhale. Danny hands me the thing he's holding behind his back.

It's the Vitruvian Man journal.

I start to open it, but he puts his hand on the cover. "Not now," he says. "It's for after I go. To remember me."

"You think I'd forget you?" All the same, as I reach my arms around him and he hugs me tight, I tell myself to remember this, remember how this feels.

"Forgot the control," Warren says, exiting the cage. I step back from Danny and stuff my hands into my lab-coat pockets. Warren grabs something from the worktable and walks back toward the cage.

"Is that a cell phone, Warren?"

"Yep."

"Whose?"

"Corban Upton's. Payback for creaming me in the chess tournament last week." He laughs like an evil madman and disappears inside.

"I'm gonna miss that guy," Danny says. "Not sure he'd say the same about me, though."

"Are you kidding? We haven't had this much excitement around here since the time we built a replica 15th-century trebuchet and launched potatoes clear over to Acoma Park." Danny smirks. "Warren won't know what to do with himself after you're gone."

And neither will I.

"Are you sure you want to go through with this?"

He closes his eyes and nods. "I need to get home. Face whatever it is that's happening there." He takes my hand and gives me a grim smile. "I'm going to miss you."

Don't cry. Don't cry. Don't. "Me too," I manage to say with only a small quaver. "Wait—" Frantically, I search my pockets. "I didn't give you anything to remember me by." And then, "Oh." Logic has left my brain. "You wouldn't be able to take anything with you anyway." My hands are shaking. I'm a mess.

He smiles and tucks my hair behind my ear. "Don't worry. I could never forget you, Eevee Solomon."

He moves to hug me again but Warren interrupts. "The device is switched on and the timer is ticking down. Here." He hands Danny a pair of goggles. "Just in case."

"Okay," Danny says, pulling the goggles over his eyes. "Let's do this." He shakes Warren's hand and we walk to the cage. Just before going inside, he turns to me, smiles and kisses me on the cheek.

I watch Warren shut the door. Watch him check the seal. I'm so lost in my thoughts, he has to ask me twice to get the clipboard so we can record results.

Warren and I move to the far side of the garage. He holds his stopwatch in front of us. One minute left to go. When it reaches zero, the timer mechanism will release the stopgap on the power connection, the device will detonate, and then . . .

"You doing okay?" Warren calls.

"Yep," Danny calls back.

My hands feel cold wrapped around the clipboard. My eyes refuse to blink, watching the numbers race down to zero. My mind, though, floods with regret, echoing again and again all the things I wish I'd said to him, things now I'll never get a chance to say.

36

Danny

There's a chair, but I can't sit still. On a wooden pallet lies a mess of copper wire and computer parts. I stay away from it, standing as close to the door as I can.

"You doing okay?" Warren yells.

"Yep," I answer, because what am I supposed to say? That I'm scared? Of leaving. Of staying. Of Eevee finding out the truth about me and Red December.

Warren's voice comes again, starting the countdown. "Three."

I close my eyes and imagine her. Dark hair. Sweet smile. If this goes bad, I—

"Two."

—want my last thought to be of her. Oh God. I don't want to—

"One."

—leave.

I press myself against the wall and wait for it. . . .

The sound of an alarm pings into the silence. I pull the goggles off. Everything inside the cage is the same, except for a simple wisp of smoke rising from the cell phone.

I'm still him. I'm still here.

The EMP went off and I'm still here.

The door rattles, opens. Warren runs in as I run out.

Eevee rushes toward me and I catch her in my arms. Hold her tight. Look at her beautiful face. "I don't want to leave you."

She smiles as Warren shouts, "The EMP worked! Corban's phone is toast!"

37

EEVEE

In the days after our homemade EMP fails to send Danny back home, I find myself leafing through the women's magazines my mother has accumulated. According to *Strut!* magazine, there are seven sure signs you're in love with another person:

1. You want to spend every waking minute with the person. (Every sleeping minute, too!)

Danny and I spend as much time together as we can. I cut out of class early or skip school altogether. He comes to my window late, after Dad has gone to bed. It's a dangerous game, but now that we're together, we don't want to waste a single minute.

2. You would give the person the world if you could.

We go to the mall one afternoon, share a pretzel and look at the window displays. He tells me how different everything is from the mall in his Phoenix. I show him the geocaches

Warren and I have found. As we walk toward the exit, we pass a jewelry cart in the center walkway, loaded with bangles and earrings, scarves and sunglasses.

"Hey, check it out." Danny points at a square pendant hanging from a leather thong. "This looks kinda like the necklace my mom gave me." He turns to the saleswoman. "How much?"

While he talks to her, I read the tag. *This necklace is structured from pure bismuth. Bismuth crystals are known for their stunning iridescent colors and unique stair-step structures.*

Danny takes the necklace down from the display and clasps it around my neck.

3. You miss the person like crazy when you have to be apart.

When we do go to school, I'm distracted. Danny is all I think about. I have a difficult time carrying on simple conversations, even with Warren (though I suspect he's happily having his own concentration issues, thanks to Missy). Sitting through classes, I struggle to focus, counting the minutes until I can see him again. Einstein called time a "stubbornly persistent illusion." He couldn't have been more right. And it's never more stubbornly persistent than those last five minutes before the bell rings.

4. You find everything the person says and does totally fascinating.

We sit side by side in the backyard, me looking at the necklace around my neck and him looking at me.

"Did you choose this one because of the fractal pattern?"

"Yes," he says, shaking his head no.

"Look at it closer." I hold the pendant out toward him. "See the stair-step formation? Everything is constructed in patterns. Leaves. Tree branches. This crystal." I let it drop back to my neck and look up at the sky. "I think even the stars must have a fractal structure. We just haven't found the right vantage point yet to see it." I take his hand and point to the creases in the curve between his thumb and index finger. "Even we have fractal patterns."

He holds his hand up to his face for a closer look. "How do you know all this stuff?"

"I don't know. I just like understanding how things work and why." I take his hand again and hold it in mine. "Your turn. Tell me something I don't know."

He makes a thinking face. "Ah. How's this? My middle name is Winchester."

"Like the gun?"

"Yep. It was my great-great-grandfather's name."

"Daniel Winchester Ogden." I smirk. "Makes you sound dangerous."

"I am dangerous." He tries to look tough, but cracks into a smile. "What about you? Why do you spell your name that way?"

"I like the symmetry of it."

He looks at me for a moment, then shakes his head. "Most people I can figure out right away. But not you." He tucks my hair behind my ear. "Not you."

5. You get jealous if anyone else makes a pass at them.

Sometimes he catches me off guard and kisses me when I least expect it. Just outside the school gates. Over homework with my dad barely ten feet away. Every kiss feels like a new, unexpected thing. And after every one, I pray that feeling never ends.

But one time he kisses me and it's different. His lips press harder, his arms hold me tighter, his hands wander.

I pull away. "Tell me. About her."

At first he looks hurt, but then he flops back on the couch and says everything I already know.

He tells me how she was. With him.

The other Eevee is so different from me. She does whatever she wants, whenever she wants. She isn't controlled by anyone.

"I can see why you like her."

He scowls. "What am I supposed to say to that?"

"Whatever. It doesn't matter."

I hate being jealous of her. I hate hating her.

Hating myself.

6. You can't imagine a life without the person.

Working on English homework at Dad's, I whisper, "Don't you think it's strange that you met me in your universe, and then just *happened* to end up next to me here in my class?"

"No," he says, not looking up from his paper. "I think it's awesome."

"I'm serious. Isn't that a bit too coincidental?" I tap my pencil on the table. Every system has an underlying order.

Every microcosm is a reflection of the macro. In an ordered system, is there room for coincidence?

Unless . . .

"What if you're a nonlinear complication in our deterministic system?"

He looks up. "Are you even speaking English?"

"If you're nonlinear here, are you nonlinear in every parallel system? But if you're consistently nonlinear, then that would make you linear." My brain starts to cramp.

He puts his pencil down and stretches. "I have no idea what you're saying."

"What if Eevee and Danny meet in every universe?"

He grins. "Sounds perfect."

7. You're happy and life couldn't be better.

38

Danny

We sit at her dad's kitchen table after dinner. Sid's in the other room, keeping an ear out, I'm sure. We've been spending all of our time together, *relishing* all of our time together. I don't know who's happier I'm still here, her or me. All that time I was fighting to get home, I never realized what I had right in front of me. I miss my family, and Germ—how could I not?— but I think if they saw me now, they'd understand. They'd want this for me, too. They'd want me to embrace this life, now that I'm here.

She taps my foot under the table. *Tap tap.* I don't look up from the textbook. This time we're reading "The Lottery" for that crazy Fish she-troll. I'm at the part where Mrs. Hutchinson finds her husband and kids in the crowd. *Tap tap.*

"Shhh."

She folds her arms on the table. I pretend not to notice her smiling up at me through her eyelashes. I turn the page. She taps my foot again.

"What? I'm reading."

She reaches out to cover the pages with her hands, but I pull the book away. "You're totally going to flunk if you don't pay attention."

"I don't care."

"You lie." I start reading again just to drive her crazy. "'A sudden hush fell on the crowd as . . .'" The words on the page blur. Static fills my head. I feel the book fall from my hands as the pulsing takes over. Through the confusion, a woman's voice.

. . . can't believe you're seriously considering this.

Mom?

Two figures emerge in the haze. I can barely make them out. But then, Dad's voice.

I don't see any other way. Do you?

I fight to push through, but that other force pushes me back.

Danny? What's wrong?

They're almost in focus. My chest goes so tight I'm gonna die. I ease up, let the pulsing pound me. Cold shivers through me, and then, there they are.

Here I am.

Kind of.

The living room walls glow. The whole place hums, shifting in and out of focus. I'm so close.

Then the force slams into me, races through me, pushes me back. My world swirls into a haze and I'm falling, flailing.

The kitchen chair catches me. My chest burns, my head spins.

I was there.

I was actually there.

Across the table, Eevee stares at me, too stunned to speak.

I'm stunned, too, and not just because it happened again. That force that pushes back? I think I know what that is. Or rather, who.

It's him. The other Danny.

39

EEVEE

And then, after six blissful, drama-free days, the storm breaks.

Danny and I walk across Mom's yard after a long day of avoiding school to spend time together. I hear Warren call my name and turn to see him running across the street, backpack bouncing behind him. His goggles are crooked and his words run together.

"Wherehaveyoubeen?"

"What?"

"Beenlookingforyouallday." He leans over and holds his knees.

"Slow down," I say. "What's wrong?"

"Mac," he says, panting. "He's gone."

"What do you mean—"

"Fired." He stands up and adjusts his backpack. "Murray fired him."

"What?!" I grab Danny's arm. "What for?"

"Rumor is, he set up an illegal lab on campus. Some are saying drugs."

I scoff. "Yeah, right."

"You know what I think?" He tries to catch his breath. "It's those guys in suits. And whatever's going on at his house. If only we'd been able to talk to him before this." He lifts his goggles to wipe his face and mutters about Mac's terrible timing for being MIA. His goggles snap back into place. "And get this: someone got past my firewall and jacked my hard drive."

Oh no. "Do you think it was because of the . . . ?"

He nods, his lips forming a thin line. "The EMP."

Still reeling, I walk through the front door and stop. Mom and Dad are seated at Mom's kitchen table, and Dad has that look on his face.

I've only seen the look two other times, once when I forgot to lock my bike and someone took it; and once when I stole Phoebe Markel's Sassy doll. My parents decided those dolls instilled the wrong ideas in young girls' minds and forbade me to play with them.

I hated giving that doll back.

"What's wrong?" I set my bag down by the couch and hear Danny shut the door behind me. Mom looks at Dad. Dad nods at Mom. Mom puts her phone on speaker and turns up the volume.

"Ms. Bennett, this is Stacy Wright, guidance counselor at

Palo Brea High School. I'm calling in reference to the recent changes in Eve's behavior. She's had some unexcused absences and her teachers have notified me of their concern about her grades. Obviously, given Eve's outstanding achievements, these changes have raised flags. Please call me back so we can set up a time to discuss this matter. Thank you."

The look on Dad's face says it all. I'm doomed.

"So tell me." He crosses his arms. "Just how many days have you been absent, young lady?"

I open my mouth to answer and my brain tumbles, trying to figure out the number. I don't even know what day it is. "Two? I think?"

He explodes. "You don't even know?!" Mom puts her hand to her mouth. "And where were you during these however-many days?"

"I . . ." I really don't want to answer the question. I don't know how. So I close my mouth and stare at my feet.

Danny clears his throat. "Mr. Solomon?"

Dad holds up his hand. "This doesn't concern . . ." Then his eyes narrow. "Danny, can *you* tell us where Eve was the days she wasn't at school?"

"She was with me, sir."

"I see."

Mom walks toward me. "Eevee, it's normal to want to express your will and push boundar—"

"Bullshit," Dad says. "What's happened to your grades, Eve?"

"I was talking, Sid."

"You were giving her an out." He turns back to me. "Your grades, young lady."

I can't look him in the eye. "I missed a test in chemistry. And I have three late assignments. Two in physics and one in history." He looks devastated. Grades are Dad's lifeblood. I scramble for something good to tell him. "But my grade in English is actually better, thanks to Danny. And I'm almost caught up on the other work."

It doesn't help. He still looks like he's going to kill me.

"Whatever's going on here . . ." He points back and forth between me and Danny. "This sneaking around. It stops now. No more."

"Yes, sir," Danny says.

"And you." He takes a step toward Danny. "I trusted you. You told me you could follow the rule."

"Sid," Mom says.

He puts his finger in Danny's face. "Eve is my daughter and I will not let her future be ruined because some delinquent—"

"Sid!" Mom yells. "That's enough. You're in my house. Sit down."

He walks toward me, his face contorted, and he says the worst thing possible. "I'm really disappointed in you, Eve. I thought we'd raised you better than this." Then he walks back to the table and crosses his arms. He doesn't sit.

"You don't know what's really going on," I say, finally finding my voice. "You don't understand."

Something I said catches Mom's attention. She takes me aside. "Honey," she whispers, "are you . . . in trouble?"

"What?"

"I mean . . ." She looks embarrassed.

Oh my God. "No, Mom." I push her arm away. "Nothing like that. It's . . ." I close my eyes. "Danny has this. Thing. Where he."

I hear the front door close. Danny is gone.

All hell breaks loose.

40

Danny

I leave. Turn away from them and walk out. Stupid, sure; but everything I can think of to say would only make it worse. The whole thing is my fault.

The skateboard feels solid under my feet and I relax a little as I ride. Maybe they'll go easier on her without me there. I'll just get some fresh air and go back later, after things have died down.

It's late. Rush-hour traffic crowds Thunderbird Road. Fiery sunspots glint off chrome and glass. I'm so wired I don't think I could sit still right now if I tried. It feels good to ride. To be out. To be moving. The city air is full of car exhaust and desert dust. This is freedom. This is the way Phoenix should feel.

I know it's a long shot, but I skate all the way to Germ's house. By the time I get there, my legs are like rubber. This time, though, it's worth it. There's a beat-up Nova in the driveway and the porch light is on. The door opens and Germ walks out of the house. Behind him is another guy I've never seen before.

My feet hit the sidewalk, leaving the board behind. "Germ!"

He eyes me as he slips a baseball cap backward over his scruffy hair. The other guy says something I can't hear and Germ shakes his head.

"Man," I say when I'm closer, "what a crazy ride."

"Yeah," he says. He takes the toothpick out of his mouth and spits in the grass. "How's it going?"

The other guy—gangly and covered in tats—starts to speak, but Germ elbows him.

"Same old." I stare at my best friend. His hair is longer, dirtier, and he's skinnier than ever. "Trying to figure some things out."

"Cool." He rolls the toothpick across his lips with his tongue. "Zinc and I were just going out. Wanna come?"

Zinc protests again. Germ shuts him up. "Would you chill, man? Be cool." Zinc turns away, annoyed. There's a name stitched onto the pocket of his work shirt: *Neil.*

The Zinc-Neil guy is twitchier than I am. And there's something in Germ's eyes. Something I can't put my finger on. Whatever. I shake off the bad vibes and go with it. "Yeah, man. I'm in."

"All right then." Germ spits the toothpick into the grass and climbs into the beater. Zinc takes shotgun. The back door sticks, but I get it open on the third try. The engine roars like a sick beast and we're off to who knows where.

Sunset blazes across the downtown skyline as Germ sails the highway overpass. A jet takes off from Sky Harbor, an orange phoenix rising from the city.

"Where we headed?" I yell to the front seat. The windows are down and the wind is fierce. As we round a curve, I slide across the vinyl seats from the center to the passenger side. A truck cuts us off and Germ lays on the horn. He's right on the guy's tail. Zinc and the other driver exchange hand signals.

"Where we headed, Zinc?" Germ asks.

"Party, man."

Germ laughs.

It's like there's a joke, and I'm not getting it. But it's okay. He may not be my Germ, but he's still Jeremy Bulman. And he knows me. I decide to test the waters, figure out where this Germ overlaps with my friend.

"You going out for swim team this year?" I ask.

They both turn around and look at me. The car lists and Germ turns back just in time to correct. "What?"

"You on the swim team, man?" Zinc asks me. He makes swimming motions with his hands, plugs his nose like he's going under.

I shake my head. Idiot.

Germ takes the off-ramp at 7th Street. Lifts his foot from the gas and the engine moans like it's tired of being whipped. He smacks Zinc across the chest with the back of his hand and points at a gas station. "Gonna stock up."

He pulls the car into an empty spot by the ice machines and leaves the engine running. "Hey, swimmy. Watch the wheels." His door slams before I can respond.

Zinc turns to me. "That means you wait here. Sit in the driver's seat so no one jacks our ride." And then he's gone, too. A lot of fun this is.

I climb over the bench seat to the front and sit behind the wheel. The seat's warm and it grosses me out. I watch Germ's baseball hat through the store's windows until he moves out of sight.

What am I doing? I should have stayed at Eevee's. This is stupid.

My head falls back against the headrest and the car rumbles beneath me. My eyes spaz behind closed lids. I try to relax, to just breathe, but the pulsing starts up and my chest goes tight. A slow static fills my head. Voices swim in and out.

Do I give up? Or fight to push through, to push harder than the other Danny? Without Eevee, what reason do I have to stay here?

The car door slams and I gasp. My eyes dart open. Someone's legs are going over the seat to the back.

"Go! Go! Kill it, man!"

I throw the stick into reverse and peel from the lot. Zinc and Germ both scream in my ears. I don't check for oncoming. Just pull out onto 7th Street going south, choking on spit and shock. Coughing, half-blinded to the road with my brain spinning.

They high-five over the bench seat. Germ whoops. Zinc howls and drums his hands on the ceiling.

As soon as I can breathe, I yell, "What the hell?!"

Germ pushes the back of my head. "Just giving you shit,

man. It's cool. Go south here until you hit Baseline. Watch your speed."

"Tell me where we're going."

"I told you. A party."

"Where?"

"What are you, my mother? Shit, man. Lighten up."

I hear the fresh pop of a can opening. Not good. I drop my speed to three under and scan the road for cops. "Put that away."

"Just be a good driver, Granny, and we'll be fine."

We only get a couple of miles south when the lights flash behind me.

Germ turns to look at the squad car and yells, "Gun it!"

My arms shake and everything moves in slow-mo. This can't be happening.

"Go! Go!"

I take my foot off the gas. Turn on my signal.

"What are you doing, man?" Zinc's hot breath is in my face. Germ pounds on my seat back and smacks me in the head. Zinc pounds his foot over mine on the gas pedal and the car jolts forward.

The sirens wail and the cop's so close I can see him calling for backup. I push Zinc's face away with one hand and steer with the other. Work to wiggle my foot out from under his. The car swerves. Stinks like beer. I plant both feet on the brake. The engine races and the tires smoke.

For a split second, I think of throwing myself out of the car, but there's no way. I can't take my foot from the brake. If I do, the car zooms forward and takes me with it. Zinc and I push each other, struggling for control of the gearshift. I shove it into neutral just as something heavy clocks me in the head. Blinking out of consciousness, I see the cop in the rearview approaching with his gun drawn.

41

EEVEE

I tell them the truth. I tell them everything.

About Danny showing up in class that day and how he came from another universe. About Warren and me trying to figure out how to help him. About Danny's nightmares that pull him away somewhere else and how we built an EMP device to try to help him get home but it failed.

They don't believe me, of course. Dad accuses me of lying, of being on drugs, of not being grateful for all they've done, giving me opportunities that others only dream of. Mom diagnoses me with depression, low self-esteem, poor impulse control, a personality disorder evidenced by self-deception. She picks up the phone to make an appointment with her shrink, but before she can dial, I do something I haven't done in years.

I raise my voice.

"I'm not a machine. You can't just feed in information and output good grades." I turn to Mom. "And you can't just start caring fifteen years too late and expect it to be enough."

It feels good to yell.

They look at me like I've lost my mind, then they lay into each other. Ten years of ugliness explodes right there in Mom's kitchen.

Instead of listening to them shout in each other's faces, I slip down the hall to my room. They just keep debating whose fault it is I'm ruining my life, accusing each other of giving me too much freedom and not enough, of letting me watch too much television and too little, of letting me eat the wrong things and read the wrong things and think the wrong things.

That's my parents, blaming Twinkies. Are the other Eevee's parents as ridiculous as mine?

I stare out my window, hoping he'll be out front but knowing he won't. Where did he go? The foster home? Will he be eating out of the garbage again? I curl up on my bed and cry.

When I can't cry anymore, and when I can't stand the yelling, I crawl into my closet and wrap the sleeves of a sweatshirt around my head to drown everything out. Suddenly I'm six years old again, ankles crossed and arms around my knees in the safety of the darkness. I hum until all I can hear is my own voice. What would the other Eve do in this situation? She wouldn't cry or hide. She would never have gotten caught in the first place.

A sound that isn't shouting or humming carries through the sweatshirt. Ringing. I let the sweatshirt fall away from my ears. The yelling has stopped, and only the phone disturbs the quiet. I slide the closet door open partway. And in the half-light, I see it.

Did you find it? he'd asked at the end of our perfect day.

I touch the pencil lines on the inside of the closet door. Danny drew us sitting knee to knee under the Canal Park overpass, surrounded by street art. Every detail is amazing, from our initials on the walls—*EV + DOA*—to our entwined hands.

It's been right there all along.

The front door slams. I crawl out of the closet and watch out the window as Dad's car pulls away. Either he's had enough, or something is wrong.

There's a knock at my door. "Eevee?"

Mom's face is pale. "That was Danny on the phone."

My stomach drops. "Where is he? What's wrong?"

"He's in jail. Your father's gone to bail him out."

"I just don't understand why you thought you had to lie."

Mom and I take turns pacing the living room, waiting for news from Dad. My eyes are so dry from crying I want to claw them out of my head. I don't have the energy to tell Mom *again* that I'm not lying, so I just say what she wants to hear. "I'm sorry."

"Honey, I was fifteen once. I know how strange it is, having all of these changes going on in your brain and body."

"*Mom, I*—"

She holds up her hand. "And I might be old, but I'm still human. I know what it's like to have a boy take interest in you."

"Mom, really, it's—"

"It's exciting. It makes you feel alive. But sometimes those feelings can cloud your judgment. Make you do foolish things."

I laugh. "Like you ever did anything foolish."

"I did. And I'd tell you about it, too, except I don't want to give you any ideas."

I raise my eyebrows. Whatever she's done, I don't want to hear it.

She sits beside me and takes my hands in hers. "Listen, I know we're not a typical family. And I know I've been too busy trying to get my new career off the ground. It's a lot to handle, especially on top of school and a social life. But whatever's going on, you can always come talk to me."

"I know, but . . ."

"But what?"

I shrug. "It's like you're always trying to fix me or change me into something I'm not."

She sits up a little straighter, surprised. "Oh." Her hands fidget in her lap. "I—I suppose I am guilty of that. I don't mean to be. It's just . . . Sometimes I'm afraid you're going to end up like me, like I was before I realized I didn't like who I'd become." She takes my hands and looks me in the eye. "I don't want that to happen to you."

"I don't either." My voice is pinched in my throat. "But maybe if you let me figure out how I am now, I won't have to change it all later."

She nods. "Less fixing, more listening. I can do that." She hugs me and for the first time in a long time, I don't fight it.

"Mom?" We both dab at our eyes. "What is Dad going to do with Danny after he's out?"

"Take him home, I suppose."

I rocket from the couch. "He can't."

"It's for the best."

"Danny's foster dad will kill him."

"He'll be CPS's worry now. They have systems in place—"

I don't wait for her to finish. I leave by the front door and she doesn't stop me.

Outside, I sit in the grass, in the spot where we'd sat that perfect night, and try to figure out how he could've landed himself in jail. He's smarter than that, even if he doesn't follow rules.

Doubts wiggle their way into my thoughts. What if he isn't who he said he is? What do I know about him, really? And the Danny I do know—the one I've known since sixth grade—well, the cops probably know him by name. I sit for a long time, feeding the doubts with all kinds of awful ideas.

Later, after the stars have shifted in the sky, headlights glare down the street. I recognize the sound of Dad's car before he turns into the driveway and kills the engine. I watch from the shadows as he walks toward Mom's.

No Danny.

I don't stick around for the fireworks. Instead, I sneak around the back of Dad's house and get Danny's bike. I have to find him.

42

DANNY

I scrawl my name across the form and hand the officer the clipboard. He drops it onto the counter and opens a plastic bag.

"One wallet." He doesn't look at me. "One pen."

There it is, the sum of my existence in this world on display for all to see. And neither actually belongs to me. I stuff the wallet and pen into my back pocket and say thanks, but the officer's already moved on to his next incarcerated loser.

Sid stands by the exit with his arms crossed, his face like a brewing storm. I didn't want to call him, but who else is there? Brent? Yeah, right. I'd end up in the morgue.

When I get close enough to talk to him, Sid turns and walks out, clanging his car keys against his thigh with each step. I follow him, expecting the door to slam behind me, but it has one of those slowing arms on it and I have to actually push it shut, then hurry to catch up. Sid's already in his Volvo. I get in and sling the seat belt across my lap, inhale to speak, but he clears his throat and starts the engine. Gives two loud revs.

Right. Okay. Silence is good. I can do silence.

Sid backs out of the space and the car pushes forward into the night. Clock on the dash reads 8:18. Three hours in a holding cell, watching my back and studying the scraped paint on the bars. A guy in the next cell was tripping something fierce. Rolling on the floor and yowling like a cat. No idea where they stuffed Germ and Zinc-Neil. I touch the knob on my head where Germ clocked me. Pull away my hand expecting to see more blood, but there's none.

God, what an idiot. What was I thinking, getting in that car with them?

The streetlights paint a slow strobe across the hood, the dash, my knees, and repeat. Sid's hands grip the steering wheel. My own are clammy. I wipe them on my jeans and clear my throat to speak, expecting him to shut me up again. But he doesn't. Instead, he just smolders.

So I do what neither of us expects.

I tell him the truth.

"I'm not from here. I'm from another universe." My voice sounds like someone else, someone not me. Sid just stares ahead, turns on the blinker, makes a right.

"See, there isn't just one universe. There are lots of them. And somehow I crossed from mine to here. We think it had to do with the EMP, but now we're not sure."

The car accelerates. Sid merges onto the freeway, heading north. The streetlights blink by.

"There's an Eevee in my universe, too, but she's not like

your Eevee. She's . . ." Adjectives race through my brain, but I stick with what's safe. "She's an artist." When he still doesn't respond, I add, "A really good one."

Sid navigates through traffic, weaving from one lane to the next, always using his blinker. He may drive fast, but he drives responsibly.

"She and Warren have been trying to help me. There's this . . . thing . . . that keeps happening, almost pulling me back to my universe, but it's like it loses its grip on me. I don't know. It's weird. But anyway, they were . . . trying . . ."

Sid passes the Thunderbird Road exit. Where is he going?

". . . Were trying to help me get back to my world. And I thought it was going to work, and the thing is . . ."

He takes the Bell Road exit and I realize where we're headed. The car sails through the green light and makes such a sharp left turn that my hand instinctively grips the door. Sid accelerates again, the needle hovering at ten over. I swallow and continue.

"The thing is, I realized I don't want to leave. I mean, I miss my family, of course. But if I go back, if I leave . . ."

Even in the dark of the car I can see the tightness in Sid's face.

"I don't want to leave her. I don't want to leave Eevee."

He swings a left onto 39th and barrels south. Slows into the final turn and eases the car to a stop. The foster home is dark. Sid stretches his fingers, keeping his palms on the wheel. The air is thick with anger. His voice holds no uncertainty.

"You stay away from her."

He doesn't look at me. Doesn't see me nod. As soon as the

car door closes behind me, he's gone. Two red-eye taillights glaring, threatening.

●

Like hell I'm staying here.

When I'm sure Sid's car is gone, I skirt the front yard of the foster house to get at the garage without being seen. I'm sure I saw an old bike there. The light from the television flickers through the window. There are voices, but I can't tell if it's Brent and Sooz talking or the people on TV. They've got to know what happened. Whatever authority monitors Danny's life must have called by now.

Or maybe not. Maybe they don't track what happens here. Maybe these kids have slipped through the system. Until I reported it, no one seemed to notice they were being bullied by that disgusting excuse for a man, and who knows whether they've done anything about it since then.

The garage door sticks when I try to lift it, and rumbles ominously when it comes unstuck. I'm trying to slide it open as slowly and softly as possible, but pressure builds in my chest and my eyes blur. No. Not now. I crouch down to keep from falling. Try to relax, to keep breathing. It feels like a car is parked on my lungs. A female voice slithers through the static.

He's one of them.

Her perfume colors blue across the haze.

Can't be caught here. I struggle to stave off the sounds and images, but it's no good. Through the haze, I hear Eevee's voice.

All the proof you need is right here.

Shapes move through a blinding light. Whatever's happening, it's bad. Real bad. I can't let this happen. Can't let it take me. Where is the other Danny? Why isn't he fighting back?

There's something hard and cold in my hand. I slam it down, feel the jolt rocket through my arm.

Lock him up.

I slam my fist down again and again until the pulsing eases and my empty fist hits the solid floor beneath me. It's dark. The smell of her perfume is gone, replaced by dirt and gasoline.

What is she doing there? Where was I?

I cough the tightness from my chest. Pull myself up using the bumper of Brent's truck. My body feels heavy, exhausted. I wait for my eyes to adjust to the dark, then reach along the wall for the light switch.

Near the shelves against the wall is a pink ten-speed. A girl's bike. Well, at least it's wheels. It'll get me where I need to go, which is anywhere far from here.

I fumble over the lawn mower, the cobwebbed high chair and rusted toolboxes. Slip the bike out of its place. Press my thumb into the wheels. They're soft but they'll get the job done.

The gears chatter as I push off. Maybe if I pedal hard enough, this bubblegum ten-speed can outrun what's chasing me.

43

EEVEE

The straps of Danny's duffel bag are still tangled around the handlebars from the last time we went out painting. The rest of it bangs against my knee as I pedal toward Acoma Park. I don't have a plan; I'm just riding through the night looking for him, forcing my legs forward, peering into the shadows, moving from one amber patch of streetlight to the next. The sidewalk winds through the park, circling the playground at the far side.

There's no sign of him.

Headlights approach. I pull the bike into the dark beneath a tree and wait. Please don't let it be my parents. Have they even noticed yet that I'm gone? The car drives on and I push off again, heading toward school. Cold stars shine down on me. Exhausted and running on adrenaline, I'm trusting my gut to get me where I need to go.

The school campus is dark, of course, and locked up tight. I didn't really think he'd go there. It was just a stop on the route. I ride past the teachers' parking lot and head north, following a loose trajectory of street names and landmarks that Danny has mentioned, hoping to find the way. The night casts everything in shadows. I pass a chain-link fence, hear a barking dog. Three streets up, there it is. The dirt yard. The dead tree.

I've found the foster home.

The curtains are drawn and the lights are off. I park the bike between two cars in the neighbor's driveway and wait. There isn't any movement at the house, or anywhere on the block.

Then the porch light flicks on. The front door opens, and a woman smoking a cigarette walks outside. She stops at the curb and looks up and down the street before taking a few more puffs. The tip glows red in the darkness. A booming voice calls out from inside the house. "Sooz!" That must be Brent. Sooz takes her time with the cigarette, then tosses what's left into the street. She turns and walks slowly back up the drive. The door closes and the light goes out.

My gut tells me Danny isn't in there. Which means I'm wasting my time.

I retrace the route back to the park, the bag banging against my knees, the paint cans rattling.

Paint cans.

My legs pedal faster as I make another pass through the park (just to be sure) and then ride south to Thunderbird Road. I hang a right through the neighborhoods, my heart thumping inside my chest, and pass the strip malls and gas stations, cruising toward the Paseo Park overpass.

Danny isn't here either.

The park is deserted. Only an occasional car rumbles across the bridge. I cross my arms over the handlebars and rest my head on them, exhaustion falling on me like a blanket. Then I let the bike crash to the sidewalk, and collapse onto the grass. I've never been so tired in my life. Not just tired. Gutted. I curl up on my side and the grass pricks at my arms. My eyes ache. I try to cry, but no tears come.

Empty.

I pick the bike up again from the sidewalk and push it under the overpass. The paint cans rattle and my eyes move to the ceiling. The bright paint glows through the shadows, the words and skulls and flowers. Beautiful impermanence.

Stillness settles over me as a terrible thought fills my mind: What if he's gone? What if he had a nightmare episode, like that last one in the kitchen, and it took him and now he's gone? For good?

I wouldn't be able to do anything to change it. But if he's gone, the least I can do is make sure the world knows he was here. I'll make my own art, for him.

With uneven steps, I lug the bag up the incline of the overpass. My feet walk across the countless images. I brace the bag with my feet, pull my shirt up over my nose like he does and press my finger to the nozzle.

44

Danny

It's as good a place as any. I couldn't go back to Eevee's house after the showdown with her parents. At least here, I'm in my element.

This body is in no shape to go on, every ounce of strength spent fighting to stay in control.

I stash the bike in a clump of bushes at the bottom of the trail. Someone will find it in the morning. Ride off with it. Give it a new life. It's a trek to the overpass and my feet trudge like bricks. Whatever this is going on inside me, it feels like it won't stop until it's done me in. Maybe I should just lie down and give up. This body is in no shape to go on. In the morning, a jogger'll find me. The cops'll haul my meat off to a cooler. They'll report it on the news. Unidentified body of a young man. John Doe. DOA.

Would it be me, though, or the other Danny? Either way, we both would probably be better off.

I drag myself to the base of the overpass and crumple to

the concrete. The paintings swirl above me. I'll just lie here and let the patterns carry me away. The hard ground bites into my shoulder blades, but I'm too tired to care.

The bridge shudders as a car drives overhead, then everything goes quiet. Just my shattered breathing.

And the sound of an aerosol can.

I lean up on my elbows and listen for it again. Squint my eyes and see a guy up in the space where the bridge meets the support. The can rattles and sprays. Rattles and sprays some more.

"Hey!" My voice is pinched. I cough and try again. "Hey!"

The hissing stops and the guy creeps into the shadows. Scared. But he doesn't run.

"I didn't mean stop," I say. "Just don't paint over the moon and her name, okay?"

The can clatters as it bounces down the incline. Crashes at the bottom and spins to a stop.

Amateur.

"Danny?"

Here come the voices again. I brace myself for the crush of pressure, the pulsing. But instead, there's just one voice.

Hers.

"Danny!"

I drag myself to my feet and see her racing down the slope. She's coming at me fast, dragging her feet to slow her descent. It takes all my strength to train my eyes on her and lock my feet to the ground.

She flies the last few feet, falls against me, and before I can even catch my breath, my arms are full of awesome.

"I've got you." I squeeze her tight and kiss her face and hair.

"I thought you were gone." Her cries echo off the overpass walls.

"I thought I was, too." I look into her eyes. "Don't let me go. Please. Don't. Let me. Go." Then my mouth is on hers and her lips taste like saltwater tears.

◉

"Turn left here."

She's standing on the wheel pegs, her arms around my neck. Even though my legs feel like freaking Jell-O, just having her near keeps me going.

We turn off 51st Avenue and head down Country Gables. Looks familiar.

"Is school that way?" I point.

"Yeah."

This is the neighborhood I ran through the day I arrived.

"This one." She points to the one-story coming up on our right. I steer up the curb and into the gravel driveway. The house is dark. "I thought teachers lived as far away from school as possible."

"Not Mac."

I lean the bike against the low fence lining the yard, and feel the pressure build. Eevee grabs my hand and hurries me to the door. She knocks and paces and knocks again. It's late. Really late. This is a bad idea. The static buzzes in my brain. I focus on her face and blink away the blurring.

"We should have done this a long time ago." Her voice is

purposeful. "We should have gone to Mac the moment you showed up." She knocks again and looks through the window, then walks away toward the side of the house. I don't know if she hears me whisper her name or hears me hitting the ground, but she's at my side as the pressure crushes down.

"No, Danny!" Her face is in mine, and I try to fight. Try. But the haze takes over as I watch her lips saying my name.

45

EEVEE

The door to Mac's shop opens, lighting up the driveway, then bangs shut and his footsteps hurry toward us. "Eevee?"

"Help." I cradle Danny's head in my lap and watch his face twist in pain.

Mac crouches beside me and checks Danny's pulse. He flips open his cell phone. "Calling 9-1-1."

"Wait. Don't." Mac looks up, surprised. "He doesn't need a doctor." I don't flinch from what I have to tell him. "He's switching universes."

The cell phone falls to the ground. Mac's eyes don't leave mine as he gropes around to find it. I can't read his face. It isn't shock or even confusion. He finds the phone and slips it into his pocket. "Get his feet."

Mac catches Danny under the arms and lifts him up. I grab Danny's legs and together we carry him inside. Mac bumps the light on with his shoulder. The front room is full of moving boxes, half-empty bookshelves and blank walls where pictures used to hang.

"What—?"

He ignores my reaction and kicks a stack of books from the couch. Danny groans as we lay him down. He claws at his chest. I kneel beside him and hold his hands.

"You have exactly ten seconds to tell me what is going on," Mac says.

I take a deep breath and remind myself this is Mac I'm talking to. Someone I can trust. Then my words run together as everything spills out for the second time that night. Maybe, unlike my parents, he'll believe me. "His name is Danny. He showed up at my house a couple of weeks ago. He's from Phoenix, but not *this* Phoenix. He's been having these episodes. He hears voices and sees things, like he's stuck between here and somewhere else. Warren and I, we've been trying to figure out how he got here. We think it had something to do with an EMP. We've been trying to find you, to tell you what's happened, but . . . Where have you been?"

"EMP? Is this why you and Warren—"

"Yes. You have to help him, Mac. *Please*."

He runs a hand through his hair and starts muttering to himself. "Your parents know about this? That you're here?"

"Yes. Well, no. Not exactly. They know about Danny, but . . . They think it's crazy . . . They think I'm lying. . . ." I trail off.

Before Mac has a chance to respond, Danny gasps and bolts upright. He stares wide-eyed at Mac, then sees me and exhales.

"You're okay." I keep my voice calm. "You're okay."

He coughs as he sits up, and touches his arms, like he's checking to make sure they're still there.

"What did you see this time?" I whisper. He shakes his head and looks away.

Mac makes a chair of the coffee table and leans in. "Follow with your eyes." He holds a finger up and Danny tracks it. "Tired?"

"Exhausted."

"Dizzy?"

"Yeah."

"I know something that might help." Mac walks to the kitchen and flips on the light. "Jumping puts an enormous strain on the body."

Jumping?

The refrigerator door closes and Mac returns with a glass of orange juice. He hands it to Danny, who chugs the juice and hands the glass back empty. "Thanks."

"You're welcome. If you keep your feet flat on the floor, it can ease the spinning. Deep breathing helps, too."

What in the world?

He asks Danny if he can walk, then helps him up from the couch. I put my arm around Danny's waist and let him lean on me. His shirt is soaked with sweat.

We shuffle down the hallway to Mac's office. "Are you claustrophobic?"

Danny shakes his head. Mac flicks on a light. The pale walls are covered in scrawled-on whiteboards and schematics. Against the near wall stands a desk strewn with books and more moving boxes, and on top of a metal table in the far corner is a glass chamber.

"What is that thing," I ask, "an electric coffin?"

"Hyperbaric chamber." Mac flips a switch, lighting up the console. "Oxygenates the cells." He opens a door at the far end of the machine.

"Like what they use for divers?" Danny asks.

"Exactly." The machine powers up. "Make yourself comfortable."

Danny squeezes my hand before climbing inside.

"It won't hurt him?" I hate seeing him lying there.

"It'll make him feel like a million bucks."

"What do *you* use it for?"

Mac adjusts the settings. "To feel like a million bucks." He presses a button, and a timer on the console begins to tick down.

"What's with all the moving boxes?" I ask. "Where are you—"

"Solomon!" Warren rushes into the room, holding our research binder in his hand. "I heard the yelling at your house and saw you leave. I've been looking for you all over— Whoa!" He turns to Mac. "You have a hyperbaric chamber?"

"I do." Mac doesn't look up from the console.

"Can I try it next?"

"No." He presses a green button and speaks louder for Danny's benefit. "All good?"

Danny gives him a thumbs-up through the little round window in the chamber door. Mac nods and turns back to me and Warren.

"Mac?" Warren's hands grip the binder tight. "Why did Murray fire you?"

Mac sighs and walks over toward us. "I haven't been fired. I'm on leave."

My mind races. "Administrative leave?"

"Something like that."

"Then why the moving boxes?"

"It's complicated." Mac closes his eyes for a moment. "I have to go away for a while."

"No." I look at Warren. This can't be happening.

"Does this have to do with those guys in suits?" Warren asks.

Mac leans back against the desk and stares up at the ceiling. "Yes. Partially." He looks at us again. "CIA. They came around asking about unorthodox experiments."

"They knew about the EMP?" I ask.

Warren's mouth falls open. "How did they find out?"

"I could ask you the same question," Mac says, one eyebrow raised. "I never turned in that science fair application. If you recall, I told you guys no. But here you two show up talking like you've gone through with it." He walks back over to the hyperbaric chamber to check on Danny.

Warren looks at me, his face harsh. "What did you do?"

"Me? You think it's *my* fault they found out?" I put my hands on my hips. "You're the one whose computer got hacked."

I glare at Warren, and he glares at me. The cartoon Tesla on his T-shirt glares, too. It's the same shirt he was wearing the day we started building the Faraday cage. The same day he had a date with . . .

"Missy." Warren groans and his head falls into his hands.

"Bivins?" Mac asks.

"You told her, didn't you?" I knew it. It's all I can do not to rip the goggles off his face.

"I didn't think she'd figure it out, but . . . Wow. She's even smarter than I thought." He looks up from his hands. "On one of our dates, we told each other our deepest secrets. She said it would be romantic. . . ."

I so don't want to hear this.

"I told her about Project DELIVR—"

"Warren," I say, through gritted teeth.

"But I told it to her in Elvish, so she wouldn't understand. Except . . ."

"She speaks Elvish." I sigh. "Your Elvish-speaking girl-friend ratted us out."

"Ex-girlfriend." His face is dark.

"Regardless of who told them," Mac says, walking over to the window, "they found out." He lifts one of the slats on the blinds and peers through the gap. "Looks like they're gone again."

"Who?"

"The spooks in the white van."

Warren and I exchange looks.

"But if we're the ones who built the EMP," I ask, "why are they after you?"

Mac lets the slat fall closed again. He turns and gives me a grim smile. The hyperbaric chamber chimes and he walks over to check the dials, leaving my question unanswered. "I wish I'd known the real reason you were researching EMPs."

Danny's eyes are closed. He looks so peaceful. "Will oxygen fix him?"

"That depends on what's wrong."

"You don't know?"

Mac shakes his head. "Not yet." He eases the numbers on the console down to zero and opens the door.

Danny climbs out and stretches. "*That* was awesome."

"Feels good, doesn't it?" Mac closes the door again and powers down the machine. "Let me guess. You're starving."

"Totally."

"How about a late-night snack? And a chat to go with it."

46

DANNY

That hyper-whatever chamber is amazing. Here it is, almost eleven, I showed up totally fried, and now I feel like I could run a marathon.

I chow down on the chips and salsa Mac's put on the table and continue telling him my story. "Next thing I know, I'm in that classroom with that crazy Fish lady glaring at me."

Mac raises an eyebrow. "You mean Ms. Fischbach."

"Right, Fischbach." I drain my can of soda and open a second. Warren's across from me, scribbling in a notebook. The dude never takes a break. He probably does word problems in his sleep.

"What day was this again?" Mac sets a sandwich on a paper towel in front of me and I tear into it. Roast beef with mustard and cheddar. My stomach groans with relief.

Warren stops writing and flips back through the notebook. "He showed up two Fridays ago."

That's all? It feels longer than that. I look at Eevee, but she's eyeing Mac.

"Huh." Mac makes a thinking face. "And you suspect it was an EMP detonation that sent you jumping? Not . . . something else."

Mac asked me, but Warren answers. "The sort of explosion he described may have propelled him across the room, but not into the next universe. There had to be some other factor to cause such a dramatic event. The energy surge from an EMP might have been what it took to escalate things to the next level."

"An EMP wouldn't affect you physically," Mac says. "Unless you had some kind of implanted device."

Warren points to the notebook. "No implants."

"And even if you did have one," Mac says, "that would hardly cause you to jump universes. Stop your heart, yes. Interuniversal travel? No. So there must be another variable."

"There's something you're not telling us," Eevee says to Mac.

"Solomon," Warren hisses.

She ignores him. "Why do you keep using the word *jump*? And how did you know the orange juice would help him?"

Mac shrugs. "I've seen a lot of inexplicable things in my time."

"Things like this?" She points at me. "We show up at your door claiming he's from a parallel universe and you're not even fazed."

Tension chokes the room. Mac sets his soda can on the table and stares at her. He looks like he's having an argument with himself.

"Clearly, he's—" Warren starts, but Mac holds up his hand.

"No, no. She's right. Good observation, Eve." He stands up

and walks to the counter. "I would have told you eventually, of course. After. But with the feds breathing down my neck, well, it just seemed easier to pack up and move on."

"Told us what?" Warren looks confused.

Eevee, though, looks hurt. "You were going to leave without telling us why?"

"It would've been better that way. Safer, at least. For all of us." He turns around to face us again. The stark kitchen light deepens the circles under his eyes. He takes a deep breath and begins. "About ten years ago, after NASA but before teaching, I worked for DART, Division of Advanced Research in Technology."

"Never heard of it," Warren says.

"Few have. The department was *above* above top-secret." Mac walks to the fridge and straightens a magnet. "Also, it no longer exists."

"What happened?"

"Our team was tasked with developing innovative methods of travel utilizing clean energy. We had our hands in everything. Gyroscope propulsion. Hovercrafts. Plasma generators. But it's when we delved into electromagnetism that things got really interesting. It started with high-speed railways. It ended with teleportation."

The pen falls out of Warren's hand. "What?"

"You heard correctly." Mac puts his hands in his pockets and meanders as he speaks. "We'd perfected our models, built the units and were all set for the first test when we ran into a roadblock. Getting the higher-ups to sign off on using a live test subject. Namely, one of the team." He pops open a can of soda and takes a drink. "Admin refused and the project went silent for about two weeks, until we couldn't stand it any longer."

We watch in silence as Mac crosses the kitchen and joins us again at the table. "Ever put your heart into something, only to have it snatched away? Well, that's what it was like for us. We wanted to see that unit hum."

"You tested it anyway," Eevee says. Mac raises the can and winks. Warren's mouth hangs open.

"So?" she asks. "Did it work?"

He considers his answer. "Yes. Mostly."

"Who volunteered to be the guinea pig?" she asks.

Mac holds out his hands. *Ta-da.*

"Wait." Warren lifts his goggles onto his forehead. "*You* teleported?"

"Which is how you know what's going on with Danny," Eevee says.

"Well, kind of." Mac takes a sip. "I only jumped from one place to another within the same universe. And I did it with the help of technology. What's happened to him is ..." He looks at me and shakes his head.

"But it's similar, right?" I ask. "The pulsing. The wonky eyes."

"Sounds like it. The system we utilized was much more stable, but stepping out on the other side, I felt exhausted, famished. Among other things."

"Yeah." I can't help but smile. Someone understands.

"How many times did you jump?" Warren looks like he's gonna pop.

"Just the one time." Mac sets the can down. "After the jump, it was pretty clear we needed to do some more calculating." He stands and puts one foot up on the seat of the chair. "There was a glitch in the restructuring sequence." He lifts the hem of his jeans and pulls down his sock. The light from the kitchen shines on the metal where his ankle should be.

Eevee and I both gasp. Warren just about falls out of his seat. "You're a robot?"

Mac laughs so hard he has to wipe his eyes with a paper towel. "Sorry to disappoint you, Warren, but I'm just a run-of-the-mill human."

"Did it hurt?"

Warren and Eevee gape at me. Okay, it was a stupid question. But his answer is surprising. "Not really, to be honest. Traumatic, yes, but not painful. When I arrived at the receiver unit, my lower legs simply weren't there." He sits down and puts his arms behind his head. "We couldn't hide the accident, of course. The bigwigs found out we'd performed an unauthorized test and the project was pulled. My colleagues and I were reassigned. Didn't last much longer there, though. I was tapped for my knowledge in electromagnetism to work on surveillance technology, but that didn't hold any interest for me and I quit." He holds the soda can with both hands and inspects the label. Lost in thought. "Got a job teaching at Palo Brea, and the rest is history. Or rather physics, I suppose. Good thing I left DART when I did. Not long after, they lost funding and the whole place was shut down."

None of us say anything for a long time. What can you say

after all that? Eevee finally breaks the silence. "What are the generators for?"

Mac shakes his head, a smirk on his face. "Nothing gets past you, does it?" He stands and stretches. "This isn't exactly how I'd planned to spend the evening, but okay. Since we're all here, baring our souls, I may as well show you."

47

EEVEE

After checking again for the white van, Mac leads the way across the darkened driveway to the shop. We follow in silence. The night, the sky, everything feels like it's spinning too fast.

Mac unlocks the shop door. After we're all inside, he closes it again and switches on the lights. We file past the nearly completed entertainment center Warren and I worked on that Saturday afternoon. Sheet metal now covers the frame we helped weld, and the doors are lined with forged scrollwork. Looks amazing. Mac keeps moving, though, and we follow, continuing on toward the off-limits back room. My heart pounds so hard I swear it's going to beat out of my chest.

"About a year ago I had this idea," Mac says, unlocking the door, "that I should try to replicate the transport technology, based on memory. Crazy, right?"

The door swings open.

"Here it is."

He switches on the light and steps back for us to enter. The blue tarp still hangs across the top and over the sides. Without being asked, we all work together to pull it down. Then we stand back and stare.

The transporter is large enough for a full-grown man to stand inside, but smaller than the entertainment center in the other room. Two curved metal walls form an oval with open sides, and the inside of each wall is covered with holes about the size of a pencil eraser. Attached to the outside of one wall is a panel of controls. Knobs and dials and monitors. I run my hand along the polished metal. It's incredible.

"Does it work?" Warren asks from the other side of the unit.

"Of course it works." Mac walks over to the control panel. "Which is why Principal Murray is so unhappy with me." When he sees our confused faces, he explains, "The receiver unit is currently housed in a rarely used storage closet at school." He turns one of the dials. "The fact that it works is also why I need to disappear. The feds are onto me. If I'm going to finish this work—and get it right this time—it'll have to be somewhere far away from here." He flips a switch, then walks to the door. "I'll be right back. Don't touch anything."

As soon as he's gone, Warren does the geekiest celebration dance I've ever seen. He grabs me by the arms and exclaims, "This is so awesome!" before going to drool over the transporter some more.

Danny stands beside me. "My mind is blown. How about yours?"

I shake my head. "It's all so . . ." Before I can put my scrambled thoughts into words, I hear the generators start up outside. Danny follows me out the door, into the main shop. Mac is already on his way back inside.

"Where are you going?" he says. "The show is in here."

We follow him into the off-limits room just in time to see him shoo Warren away from the controls. Mac pulls out his cell phone. "I set up the receiving unit with remote technology so I can control it from here." He presses his finger to the screen and types with his thumbs. "There we are." He turns a dial on the console. The transporter hums louder and blue lights pinprick the inside panel.

Danny's grip on my arm startles me. One look at his face and I realize what's happening.

He's jumping.

"No!" I grab him by both arms. "Mac!" I yell. "Turn it off!"

Mac sees Danny's reaction and races back to the control panel. The lights of the transporter dim and the hum quiets until the only sounds in the shop are the rumble of the generators and Danny's ragged breathing. I watch his eyes until they focus on me again, then wrap my arms around him.

Mac stands still, like he's so lost in thought he's forgotten how to move. "Can't be. Not possible." He pulls a records log from a nearby cabinet and scans the pages. "And yet, there it is." He presses his finger against the log entry. "The first successful transmission happened two Fridays ago. A Macintosh apple left this shop and materialized in the utility closet at Palo Brea. The same day he jumped universes."

"Maybe it's a coincidence." Even as I make the suggestion, though, I realize I don't believe in coincidences. Not anymore.

Back in the house, Mac paces the living room while Danny recovers on the couch. He looks like a train wreck, his face so pale it scares me.

"Clearly the transporter is causing some kind of disturbance," Mac says. "But what kind? And more importantly, how?"

Warren flips through the pages of his notebook. "Could it be a wormhole?"

Mac continues to pace, considering Warren's suggestion. I lean over to Danny and whisper, "Did you see anything that time?"

He shakes his head. "Not now."

I wish he'd just tell me. Like anything would surprise me at this point.

"Wormhole . . . wormhole . . ." Mac stops pacing and holds up his hands like he's imagining a large picture on the wall. "If I could just . . . Then we'd . . ." He snaps his fingers. "Be right back."

He disappears down the hall, then yells, "Warren! Come give me a hand."

After some banging noises and a small crash, the two slide a whiteboard into the living room. They lift it onto the loveseat and secure it at the corners with stacks of books.

"This is more like it." Mac uncaps a marker. "Can't think without a pen in my hand." He draws a green line down the center of the board. At the top of one side, he writes DANNY and on the other, TRANSPORTER. "Now," he says, turning back to us, "if we can figure out the correlation between Danny and the transport system, perhaps we can find a way to send him back home."

"How about to keep me here?" Danny asks.

Mac looks surprised. "Is that what you want?"

"Yes." Danny's face looks strained, but he squeezes my hand. "If I can."

Mac nods, his fingers uncapping and recapping the marker. "Well, then. Appears we have our objective." He turns back to the board. "Let's generate some theories."

48

Danny

Just after midnight, the whiteboard is full of scribbled words and symbols. One side is about me, my symptoms, my jump here. Mac writes on the other side, which is all about the transporter and how it works. "As you can see," he says, "while it's a complex system, the process of teleportation is really quite straightforward." He writes WORMHOLE across the green line separating the two sides and finishes with a question mark. "But how it could possibly cause a reaction resulting in Danny jumping worlds is not—"

"Incredible," Warren says. "I can't believe the government destroyed such technology."

Mac waves the marker like a scolding finger. "Not destroy. Defund. There's a big difference. I doubt the government ever disposes of anything."

Eevee sits on the edge of the couch beside me, leaning forward on her elbows. Her face is serious, still. If we weren't trying to figure out the mysteries of the universe right now,

I'd grab a pencil and draw her. Instead, I etch her image in my brain. The way the light hits her cheek and casts shadows down her neck. The way her hair spills over her shoulder. How her eyes can change from intense to playful so fast it gives me whiplash.

The other Eevee was all intensity. Sure, our encounter at the museum only lasted a few minutes. But there was an edge to her, a hardness that I haven't seen in this Eevee sitting here. Which explains why that Eevee had no problem turning me in to the authorities.

Maybe I should just tell her what I saw in the last jump, about the other her.

I reach over and tuck her hair behind her ear. She turns to me and smiles, but goes right back to theorizing with Mac and Warren. How would she react? What good would telling her do? It would crush her to know the other Eevee betrayed me. It's best she doesn't know. At least not about that.

"The connection must be electromagnetism." Eevee points at the whiteboard. "The EMP. The transporter. Both involve electromagnetics. That's got to mean something."

"But the EMP happened in his universe," Warren says from the moving box he's using as a chair. "Why would electromagnetism there affect our world here?"

"Well, it affected *me*," I say. "And I'm *here*. Maybe it carried over somehow? Maybe I brought it with me?"

"Electromagnetism changes how electrons behave," Warren says. "Is it possible the EMP affected his electrons, and the motion of traveling from there to here continued that effect?"

"Movement," Mac mutters, staring at the whiteboard and

tapping the capped marker against his chin. "Movement." His eyebrows lift. He writes WAVES on the board and doodles scientific symbols as he continues to speak. "Electromagnetic waves carry the vibration of an electric charge from one atom to the next. What if the electromagnets in the transporter are creating waves powerful enough to disrupt our gravitational field?"

"Warping the fabric of space-time," Warren says. "Cool."

Mac doesn't respond. He's looking at me. "We're talking about parallel realities here. Parallel universes. Danny, are you aware of anything like this happening in your world? Anything in the news about electromagnetism or issues with gravity?"

I think back to my world, two weeks ago, before everything turned upside down. The familiar fears about my family, Germ, the other Danny begin to creep in, but I push beyond that, try to focus on the stuff going on in the background. When was the last time I even watched TV? I shake my head. "I can't think of anything. But then, I don't really watch the news. It's not very reliable."

Warren rolls his eyes. Eevee kicks his moving box.

"It's okay," Mac says. "I just didn't want to overlook anything." He returns to the whiteboard.

"You okay?" Eevee whispers.

Fear continues to bleed in through my defenses. "Just thinking about home."

She squeezes my hand.

"If that's the case," Mac says, "if the transporter is warping the fabric of space-time . . ." He draws two parallel lines horizontally. "It's possible that wave pattern is causing the two worlds to connect." He erases a section of the top line and redraws it so it dips down, touching the bottom line.

His eyes are distant, the wheels in his head turning. "And what's another name for an opening or connection in space-time?"

With the red marker he circles the word WORMHOLE.

49

EEVEE

Who would have ever guessed the discovery of wormholes between parallel universes would happen in a science teacher's half-packed living room in the suburbs of Phoenix, Arizona?

Ironically, it's Warren who's now arguing that wormholes can't possibly be the answer. Mac deflects each objection with his own counterpoint. Watching them is like watching a seat-of-the-pants tennis match with a volley that just won't end.

With a groan, Mac runs a hand through his hair and stares up at the ceiling. "Listen, it's two a.m. We have a long way to go yet. Let's take ten and regroup." He caps the marker and goes to the kitchen. Warren follows.

Danny sits with his arms crossed, his jaw tight. What is he thinking about? He startles a bit when I put my hand on his knee. "Want to get some air?"

"That sounds good."

We walk through the kitchen, where Warren and Mac are still debating, out to the back patio. The light just reaches the shadowed shop building where the transporter is locked away. Where will Mac go to finish his work? Will he ever come back? I shiver, either from the thought of never seeing Mac again or the fact that my body thinks anything under 70° is cold.

Danny wraps his arms around me and rests his chin against my forehead. "I need to tell you something."

"You built a transport device, too?"

The sound of his laugh comes from deep in his chest. "No. It's something else."

More revelations? I'm sure he can feel my heart pounding.

"The morning of the explosion," he says, his arms warm around mine, "Germ and I weren't at the mall just to skate and see a parade. We were there doing a job. For Red December."

"What?" I step back. "You mean, you blew up . . ."

"No." He shakes his head. "We didn't know anything about that. We just helped them spread their propaganda through graffiti, though I guess that's bad enough. Friday morning was our last gig for them. We were tagging buildings when the bombs went off." He exhales slowly. "I think they set us up to get caught. Or worse."

The pieces fall into place. "And now Danny—the other Danny—is taking the blame."

"I'm scared, Eevee. I'm afraid to go back. I'm afraid to stay here." His jaw muscles flex. "I'm afraid you're going to hate me now that you know what really happened."

"Hate you?"

"Yeah." His face is grim. "Your boyfriend is a suspected terrorist."

Boyfriend. The word shocks me like a jolt of electricity. For a second I forget what we're talking about.

"But I'm not," he says.

"You're not?" Not my boyfriend or a terrorist?

"No." He shakes his head, his eyes wide and intent on mine. "I didn't know what Red December was up to. I swear."

Oh, good. Not a *terrorist*. My head spins. I'm out of my league here. How do other girls handle this stuff? I look at his face and realize I know one thing for sure. "I don't think I could ever hate you, Danny Ogden."

His shoulders relax like he's unloaded a huge weight. He takes hold of my hands. "Eevee, if we can't fix this thing happening with me—"

"But we will."

"Okay, but if we don't—"

"We will."

He puts his hands on my shoulders, leveling his eyes with mine. "Listen. If we don't. If I end up going, I'll try to find a way back. From there." He rests his forehead against mine. "I promise."

The odds are against him—against us—but if there's even a slim chance, I'll take it.

⬤

Mac and Warren are already at work when we get back to the living room. Did they even take a break?

"What we have to figure out," Mac says, "is why only *he* went through the wormhole."

"So you two have agreed that's what it was?" I ask, taking my seat again on the couch next to Danny. "A wormhole?"

Warren makes a face. "We've tabled the discussion for the time being."

Behind him Mac mouths, *It's a wormhole*. I try not to smirk, but Warren sees my face and turns back to see what he missed. Mac continues like nothing happened at all. "Theoretically speaking, if you could isolate a wormhole—"

"But—" Warren interrupts.

Mac holds up a hand. "I know. Logistics. Just hear me out. If you could isolate a wormhole and"—he holds one hand like he's dangling a string and the other hand cupped below—"suspend a neutron star above the entrance, the gravitational effects would be great enough to suck a person through to the other side. Assuming they survived the spaghettification, the person would have just traveled through time."

"But that's time travel," I say. "This is different."

"Well . . ." Mac holds up a finger. "Yes and no. If what we're dealing with is a wormhole between universes, who's to say it couldn't work the same way?"

Now I'm the incredulous one. "But if his world is being influenced by a neutron star, wouldn't people have noticed?"

"And it doesn't resolve the issue of only him going through," Warren says.

"True," Mac says. "But let's not give up on this yet. What do we know about stars?"

Warren answers first. "They're made of hydrogen, helium, carbon, oxygen."

"Good," Mac says, writing on the board. "Also, nitrogen.

Trace amounts of heavy metals." He adds the words CHRO-MIUM, CADMIUM, IRON, then stands back and we all look at the board.

"My dad used to teach me about stars," Danny says, and I think back to the night of our perfect day. "He said the stuff that's inside stars is the same stuff that's inside us." He looks at the three of us, then shrugs. "I thought maybe that could be . . ."

Warren begins to dismiss him, but Mac holds up a hand. "Hang on." His eyes move like he's reading formulas in the thin air. "Now, that's an interesting thought, Danny."

"You mean, my dad is right?" Danny asks.

"He could be," Mac says, scribbling again on the board. "What if the EMP somehow affected those elements—that star stuff—inside you, causing you to generate the gravitational pull needed to move through the portal between our worlds?"

I look at Danny, this boy who stepped out of nowhere and landed on my doorstep. "So, you're saying he *is* the neutron star?"

"I'm not saying it," Mac says. He points at Danny. "*He* is. Let's give credit where credit is due."

Warren scoffs. "That's impossible."

"Is it?" I think back to the day Warren handed the note to Missy during physics. "In class, the apple levitated as a re-action to the force of the electromagnets. Your transporter uses the same system, but requires an anti-gravitational force. We know Danny is affected by the jumping, that something happens to him physically, right?"

"God, yes," Danny says to me. "It feels like my insides are on fire."

Mac holds his head with both hands. "What if that burning he feels is an internal fusion reaction? Could that be our answer? Stop the reaction, stop him from jumping."

"But what if we can't?" I ask. "When a neutron star runs out of fuel, it collapses in on itself. Goes supernova and creates a black hole. What would that do to him?"

His face falls. "I don't know."

"Maybe we can neutralize it somehow." I realize I'm standing. "Maybe if we can switch it off, the reaction will find equilibrium."

"Neutralize?" Warren says. "How do you fix a dying star?"

Of course. You don't.

"All of this is ridiculous," Warren says, waving his hands at the whiteboard. "How could a neutron star exist *inside of a person*? It's highly unlikely that Danny contains most of the heavy metals found in stars, let alone enough to sustain such a reaction."

"Most of the pieces are there," Mac says. "But you're right. Is any of this even possible? Short of cutting Danny open to see how he ticks, all we have is a theory."

The thought of cutting Danny open horrifies me, so I change the subject. "If he's generating his own gravitational pull, then why didn't his whole body jump?"

"Another good question." Mac crosses his arms and studies his drawings. Finally, he says, "Perhaps his body is acting like its own kind of transporter, delivering only what's inside." He stops and considers what he just said. "Ah, now that's an interesting thought, isn't it? In the transporter, a person steps their entire body inside the machine and their whole body travels. But if the body *is* the transporter, then only a portion of the person would jump."

"Which portion?" Danny asks.

"Whatever it is that makes you you."

None of us respond. Seems like we're entering philosophical territory, a final frontier of sorts for Warren and me.

"I'm not sure what to call it," Mac says, using a red marker to circle the stick-figure Danny on the whiteboard. "But I think the EMP caused a breach between Danny's body and his consciousness, for lack of a better word. His whatever-it-is that makes him who he is."

Warren snorts. "That's just—"

"Brilliant," I say, stopping to let the theory sink in. "But we still haven't pinpointed why this happened to Danny and not everyone in range of the EMP that morning."

50

DANNY

We're all staring at the board, like we have been all night, and suddenly, instead of the markings looking like Sanskrit to me, it makes sense. Like that box drawing that flips when you change how you look at it. All the words scribbled on the whiteboard fall together and there's the answer right there.

"Paint." I point at the whiteboard. "The ingredients. Chromium? Cadmium? All of those things listed are used in paint."

"How much exposure did you have?" Mac asks. "Are we talking a daily occurrence?"

"Easily."

"Do you wear a mask? Gloves?"

"Depends on where I am. Sometimes a bandana. Sometimes just my shirt pulled up. Gloves are hit-or-miss." I sit forward on the couch. "Doesn't really matter, though. Paint always gets everywhere."

"Interesting," Mac says. "If you've been steadily exposed to these elements, breathing them in, absorbing them through your skin, then perhaps they've accumulated in your system over time. All the elements are in place. Tinder for the fire, so to speak."

"But what started the fire?" Warren asks.

Eevee shrugs. "The EMP."

He shakes his head. "No, there's something else. Something we've missed." He flips through the pages of his notebook. "An EMP is magnetic. Not incendiary. Why would an electro-magnetic pulse result in combustion, inside of only him?" He studies the diagrams on the whiteboard, then looks at me as if the answer should be written on my forehead. "What made the EMP energy focus differently on him than on everyone else?"

"You mean the paint's not enough?" They're all lost in thought.

"Focus . . ." Eevee drums her fingers on her knee. I watch her fingers moving and try to breathe through the tightness creeping across my chest.

"Could it have been some kind of electrostatic charge?" Warren asks Mac. "That could trigger pyroelectric fusion."

Eevee continues to think out loud, her lips moving, her voice soft. "We focus light with lenses. Crystals. Lasers use photonic crystals." She stops drumming and her jaw drops as her hand goes to the neck of her shirt. "Pyroelectric. Crystals. Bismuth. He was wearing a—"

Static slams through my head, drowning out Eevee's voice, drowning out the room.

No. Not now. We're so close.

I see her turn toward me, see her face twist with fear.

Pulsing pounds me and the room hazes to white. My mouth opens but all I can get out is "Eve." The other Danny doesn't push back at all, and I'm too weak to fight the pull on my own.

The other world fills my eyes. They're coming for me. My only option is to run.

51

EEVEE

Before I even realize what's happening, I'm out the door, screaming after him.

"Danny?!"

I find him cowering in the shadows on the far side of Mac's Jeep, his face staring up at nothing. I grab him by the shoulders. The gravel digs into my knees. "Danny, look at me. Look at me. Please." I pull him to me and look up at the sky, too, at the stars overhead. Tears stream down my temples and pool in my ears. I don't care. I don't care about the sky or the stars or science or myself because all I want is for him to be here and to be okay.

From his throat comes a raspy sound. Then, my name. "Eevee."

I pull back to look at him, my hands still gripping his shoulders. His eyes are like glass. Does he see me?

"Danny." I shake him. "Come back. Come back to me." I hear the door slam. Hear Mac and Warren run across the gravel. I scream at them to help, but they're as useless as I am.

For a split second, his eyes clear and his hands reach up to grab my arms. "You," he whispers. Then they cloud over again. A violent shiver goes through him and he crumples into a ball.

Time stops. No one moves.

No one even breathes.

Then Danny gasps, tilts his head up, blinks. He glares at me, confused, and I can tell from his eyes it isn't him. He looks past me at Mac and Warren. At the house, the street. At himself.

He stumbles two steps forward.

And he runs.

52

DANNY

I land with a jolt and gasp for air. My head feels heavy. The roaring in my ears fades and all I hear is the sound of my breathing.

Maybe if I don't open my eyes it won't be true.

Far off, I hear the sound of a closing door. Of footsteps getting closer. They've found me.

My eyelids open just enough to let the blinding light in. The world buzzes in white. This body feels familiar. Fits right. I inhale and feel the cold air fill my lungs. Stretch my neck and know how the muscles will move.

I'm me again.

The footsteps stop outside the door. I let my eyelids open, squinting until the room comes into view. Blank white like an empty canvas. Give me a rattle can and I'd do a job on this place. Paint it until the walls ran so black they'd never come clean.

The door slides open with a *whoosh* and she walks into the

room. Her heels *click-click* across the polished floors and her perfume filters through the air.

I look her dead in the eye. The one who turned me in. The one who landed me in this place.

Eevee Solomon.

53

EEVEE

Chaos theory states that systems run through cycles as a way of reaching equilibrium, adapting to accommodate for each variance.

An unexpected hailstorm blankets the Arizona desert in white. Drivers skid on the roads. Children are late for school. Meteorologists have an unusually busy day. Then the system adapts and life returns to normal.

Sometimes, though, a variance is introduced that is so disruptive the only way to achieve equilibrium is dynamically, setting the system into a pattern of continual adaptation.

A scientist warps the fabric of space-time, allowing a boy with a supernova heart to break the bounds of his universe. The system bounces from situation to situation and life never settles down.

The day after Danny jumped, Warren and I went back to Mac's house. The place was locked up and his car wasn't in the drive. Taped to the front door was a notice that read:

WARNING. THIS BUILDING IS UNSAFE. DO NOT OCCUPY. We searched around for clues about what happened. While we still couldn't see through the blacked-out shop windows, the generators were gone and the gravel was rutted with footprints and tracks. We asked a few of the neighbors if they'd seen anything, but no one would talk to us. Clearly, someone had been moving heavy equipment; but was it Mac, or the feds? What if DART still exists, and they found out about his transport success? Maybe they're the ones who confiscated everything and shut Mac down.

I just can't believe he's gone.

Every day I try to adapt, to figure out the new normal. It's crazy, when you think about it. Danny wasn't even here a full three weeks, but in that short time, he changed everything. Now I have to learn how to live without him. For the rest of my life.

I'm learning how to hide the pain. Pretend it doesn't exist and no one will notice. Nothing to see here, move along. Go through the motions as if everything is the way it's supposed to be.

"I'm thinking cell regeneration in lizards." Warren swaps textbooks between his locker and backpack.

"How many times do I have to tell you, Warren? No animals."

"I'm just messing with you." Smirking, he closes the locker door, then zips up his backpack and hefts it over his shoulder.

Campus is dead. No one sticks around on Friday afternoons. I think the teachers race the students to get out of here first.

It's taking him a while to get over the hurt of Missy narcing on us. I'm not sure I'm over it yet, and I wasn't even the one dating her. When Warren confronted her about it, she confessed to telling Principal Murray what we were up to. Murray, in turn, grew suspicious, found the transporter unit and got the feds involved. When Warren asked her why, she said she wanted to upset our chances of winning the science fair. That's the hardest part to take. All this loss and heartache just because of her jealousy. I made Warren swear to never, *ever* share our secrets with any future girlfriends. He agreed, but also said he would absolutely make certain that the next girl he dates doesn't speak Klingon.

"Your temperature-variation idea wasn't so bad," Warren says.

"Oh, I don't know." I adjust my own bag, heavy with homework. "The whole thing seems kind of silly now, doesn't it? Maybe we should just skip this year. Not really the same without Mac, you know?"

"Skip the *science fair*?"

"Okay, calm down. It's not like I asked you to sell your sea monkeys." The sidewalk ends and we walk through the teachers' parking lot, toward the east gate.

"Sea monkeys," he says under his breath. "What if we crossbreed sea monkeys and test if the new generation swims faster than their progenitors?"

"Aren't sea monkeys animals?"

He groans.

We bicker, talk science, then bicker more all the way home. We're almost to our street when he stops short.

"Close your eyes."

I close them and wait.

"Okay. Open them."

He holds out a small white flower.

"What is this for?"

He shrugs. "To make you smile."

I take it with both hands and smell the sweet perfume. "Thank you."

Walking again, he says, "I know it's been hard for you since he jumped."

"I'm doing okay." I don't tell him that I dodged Danny—the other Danny—today by hiding in the girls' bathroom. How I gripped the sink to keep from falling apart and told myself again and again it wasn't him.

Warren hops onto the lava rock. "Well, if you need to talk or whatever . . ."

"Thanks." He's making such an effort. Touchy-feely isn't Warren's thing, and the fact that he's even offering shows what an awesome friend he is. Deep down, though, I'm sure he knows I wouldn't actually take him up on it. "Meet you back here in the morning?"

"Yep." He holds up the Spock sign. "Fletcher, out." He jumps off the rock and walks into his house.

Inside my own, Mom waves from the computer. She points to the phone at her ear, then makes the same hand move like it's talking. She covers the phone and whispers, "Almost done."

I shake my head and whisper, "It's okay." I'm not really in the mood to talk. Sometimes I sit in my closet, stare at the drawing of us and remember. Other times I paint fractals on my walls. Today, though, I walk through the living room, into the kitchen and out to the backyard.

When I got home that morning, after Danny jumped, I found a paper on the stove held in place by the pepper grinder. Dad had created a contract. Little black bullets outlined his expectations of me: how my future would be, where I was allowed to go, who I was allowed to see, what my priorities would be and the consequences if I stepped out of bounds. At the bottom of the page were three lines. One held the half-print, half-cursive mash-up of my father's signature. The other two were meant for Mom and me. But across the paper, Mom had drawn a big X and written a note: *I'll take care of this, Eevee.*

Things are still pretty tense since Danny left. Mom and I talk more, but there's a sharp edge between the three of us—especially between me and Dad—that wasn't there before. They know I have a will of my own. More importantly, I know it.

Under the mesquite tree, I pull the Vitruvian Man journal out of my backpack and flip through the pages. He filled it with stories from his world and memories of our time together. Drawings of the places we went and the things we saw. Even this tree I'm sitting under. Pages and pages filled with his feelings for me, peppered with stars cut from paint-sample cards of purple, magenta and green.

My fingers touch the necklace. What happened when he went home? Did he find the other me? I hate not knowing.

Most girls my age are trying to figure out who's going to ask them to the prom. My boyfriend lives in another universe. I don't even know if that means we're still together. . . .

I started a new hobby: studying multiverses. It's amazing reading theoretical texts and science journals, knowing other universes really *do* exist. One theory states that parallel universes are layered on top of each other, occupying the same space, but buzzing at different frequencies. That one aligns closest with the theory we devised at Mac's. What if Danny's universe is right here, all around me? What if he's sitting next to me, as close as my breath, but neither of us knows it?

I pull my knees up to my chest and try to imagine him there, leaning against me, but all I feel is the rough bark of the tree.

The results of his blood work arrived a couple of days after he was gone. They confirmed our suspicions: elevated levels of cadmium, titanium and bismuth, as well as unusual amounts of copper, cobalt and iron. The elements of paint. The elements of stars.

For a while I obsessed on our theory of electromagnetism, the wormhole, the neutron star. Were we right? Did the bismuth necklace—a crystal with pyroelectric properties—focus the energy of the EMP, causing a fusion reaction in the built-up elements inside Danny? Did the electromagnetic waves open a wormhole that allowed him to travel between our two worlds? I wrote up a thesis, complete with diagrams. Everything looked solid on paper, but there's no way to test it. The transporter is gone. My test subject is back in his universe. Short of building my own transport system, I have nowhere to begin. I'm even fresh out of apples.

I turn the journal to the drawing of us under the stars. Our perfect day.

It could have been a perfect life.

My only consolation, strangely, is that maybe his world is in constant adaptation, too. And maybe that adaptation will lead him back.

He promised he'd try.

I hug the journal to my chest and look up through the branches to the blue sky beyond. There's a boy out there, somewhere, who loves me.

Maybe that's enough.

ACKNOWLEDGMENTS

Writing is a strange matter. Sometimes I wonder if it doesn't look like a form of mental illness: the time alone, the staring off into space, the pacing, the talking to oneself. This makes me all the more grateful to those who helped me during the writing and publishing of *Now That You're Here.*

Thank you to Katherine Harrison for your incredible vision, guidance, humor, and appreciation of science. Thank you to Isabel Warren-Lynch for your stunning cover design. Thank you to the entire team at Knopf for saying yes to my manuscript and transforming it into something far greater than I ever imagined.

Thank you to Quinlan Lee for your endless enthusiasm and encouragement, and to the Adams Literary family for welcoming me into the fold.

Thank you to James Sallis, my mentor and friend, for sharing your wisdom and teaching me the fine art of people watching. The next cup is on me.

Thank you to the Parking Lot Confessional (S. C. Green and Amy McLane) for years of camaraderie and for enduring all of those dreadful early drafts.

Thank you to Dana Hinesly, Karen North, Nannette White, Natalie Veidmark, and Heather Wiest for your friendship and constant support.

Thank you to Lin Oliver, Steve Mooser, and the self-less champions of SCBWI. Thank you to the SCBWI gang, including Sara and Tony Etienne, Kimberly Sabatini, Allan Mouw, Jeff Cox, Amy Sundberg, Jodi Moore, Ryan Dalton, Greg Pincus, and Mike Jung.

Thank you to my fellow authors in the debut Class of 2k14.

Thank you to the Thursday-night group past and present, including Michael Greenwald, Marty Murphy, Kate Cross, Kim Miles, Nanor Tabrizi, Jonathan (the Younger) Bond, Jonathan (the Elder) Levy, Kurt Reichenbaugh, Brent Ghelfi, Hirsch Handmaker, Joe Weidinger, Ray Carns, and Pat Rudnyk.

Thank you to The Ghuls (Trish, Nancy, Kavita, Irene, Angie, Frango, Chelle, DeeeeDs, and Anna) for the adventures, the laughter, the appreciation of good music and pretty shooooz.

Thank you to my parents and my family for your love and prayers, and for accepting me for the quirky girl I am. Thank you to Zoe and Cooper, for being an endless source of joy and inspiration. And thank you to my husband, Jim, for believing in me long before I believed in myself.

Finally, thank you, Readers. We live in a world of distraction, where time has become a precious commodity. Thank you for spending yours reading this book.

Turn the page for a sneak peek at

DUPLEXITY, PART II

while you were gone

Danny

The slamming door sends a thousand sound-shards through my brain. Hello, hangover. I grit my teeth and lean against the garbage can. When the ringing stops, I scuff across the front yard, shoes kicking up clouds of dirt. The sun's too damn bright. Each step feels like metal scraping the bones of my neck.

Brent's work truck growls behind me. He revs the engine a couple of times before pulling out of the driveway. I keep walking down the sidewalk, eyes forward, putting one foot in front of the other. This is the game we play. Who will blink first? When the engine's so loud my head feels like it'll split in two, I turn to face him.

A wall of sound rushes at me as tires take over the sidewalk. He lays on the horn.

Come on. Hit me. Mow me down.

But the truck swerves, bounces as it lumbers back into the street. The loose muffler swings, belching out blue exhaust.

Brent flips me off, gunning the engine and speeding away. At the corner he turns. I watch until he's out of sight, listen until the engine is gone, too.

One day he'll do it. But not today.

At the end of the block, I go the opposite direction, and the sun hits me full in the face. I check my jacket pockets, but my sunglasses are back at the house. No way I'm going back there. Not until I have to. I find some shade, pull the pack of smokes from my pocket and light one up. My head rushes with the first drag. The block wall holds me up while I wait for the nicotine to chase away the pain.

So now the big question is: put up with school, or find some better way to spend the day?

Suzy's words echo in my head: If you ditch again, they're gonna suspend you. And don't think for a second he won't find out.

The last time the school called, he pinned me down, pressed that damn cigar into the back of my arm, told me he better never hear about me stepping out of line again. Later, Benny wouldn't come near me. He said he was scared because when Brent was on me, I sounded like an angry dog. It took two whole days for Benny to trust me again, even though I told him I wasn't angry. Not with him, at least.

It's bad enough us older fosters have to live in that place, but a little guy like Benny? It's not fair.

I suck down the last of the cigarette and flick it into the gravel at the side of the road. If I'm going to school, I better get walking.

By the time I get there, English is in full swing. Ms. Fischbach stops talking when I open the door and a sea of faces stare at me.

Don't look at them. Don't think about their perfect, crap-happy lives.

My stupid shoes squeak against the floor. I walk to the empty desk near the back corner. Fischbach says, "Turn to page 774 in your anthology."

Her mouth is wide like a frog's and her voice makes my ears bleed. The only way to survive her class is to sleep. With my head on the desk and my arms folded around, I can block out most of the sound. There's still the shuffle of backpacks, the dull thud of books landing on desks. Obedient lemmings. Kissing ass in exchange for grades. Need to make Mommy and Daddy happy. Someone starts reading—that kid with the stutter. He's like a car engine that won't turn. I pull my arms tighter around my head and wait for sleep. Breathe in and out. My breathing sounds like ocean waves.

Out of nowhere, cold rips through me. Like freezing water filling my lungs. I try to lift my head, but I'm pinned down, paralyzed. A freight train roars through my head. Stars swirl behind my eyes. The desk is gone, the floor. I can't fight the force, pulling. I'm falling, kicking. There's no end to the emptiness.

So this is dying.

I let go. Give myself over to the dark.

EEVEE

The doors close and the elevator begins its slow climb to the top. I smooth my hair, watching my reflection in the metal.

Vivian's words followed me all the way from school. *Did you hear? Bosca thinks I should apply to Bellingham. Isn't that great?*

Great? Great would be Vivian's dad getting transferred to Washington and taking her with him. Great would be having some room to breathe.

What if we both end up at Bellingham? What if she gets in and I don't?

It's not that I don't like Vivian. I mean, we've been friends for a long time. Our dads were both elected to the Senate the same year. We pretty much grew up together attending state dinners, special sessions, press events. There just aren't many girls who know what it's like being the daughter of a government official.

But after Dad was elected governor, suddenly there was this unspoken thing between us. My family took the spotlight. I sat at the head table instead of on the main floor. I was interviewed for magazines and television, at first for being the governor's daughter, but then for being an artist. It was at my first gallery showing that she told me she'd decided to be an artist, too. Like it was as simple as choosing which pair of shoes to wear. She got approval from the education panel to switch from humanities to fine arts at Biltmore Elite. She's in all of my art classes, attends the same studio, interns with Bosca. It's like I can't paint anymore without her right there, looking over my shoulder.

And now she's trying to hijack Bellingham, my ticket out of here.

I close my eyes, take a deep breath and let it out. Focus on what I can control. Next week is my second gallery exhibit. Circumspect will blow people away. Everyone will rave about my paintings. Bellingham will beg me to apply. By this time next year, I'll be so far ahead of Vivian Barnes, she'll never catch up.

The elevator chimes the fourteenth floor and my reflection slides away with the doors. My steps softened by the plush carpet, I pass paintings depicting Arizona's past. Arrival of the first settlers in wagons. Migrant farmers in citrus fields. Trade with Native American tribes. The battle of Cabeza Prieta that led to the fabled Outbound lands. Did those artists hope to leave their mark, too? Most of the paintings aren't even signed.

I slip through the East Room's double doors. The curtains are open. The dull light of a gray morning filters through the windows. A vase of spider mums casts a soft shadow across the top of the baby grand. Lucinda's touch, no doubt.

Jonas drove here way too fast, even though I told him to

take his time. As usual, he barely acknowledged me, aside from opening the car door and getting my bags from the trunk.

My heels click on the marble floor, echoing into the high ceilings. Sweet, sad piano. I sweep my fingers across the glossy finish before sitting on the bench and resting them lower on the keys. Mom used to play in college, but that was a long time ago. As far as I know, I'm the only person who ever touches this beauty. And that's only on visiting weekends.

Winston's *February Sea* begins with soft, slow arpeggios and the repeating low G. I always start too quiet, afraid of breaking the silence. As if anyone will hear me. The bedrooms are over on the opposite side of the executive tower, with too many boardrooms between to count. Seven measures in, I press the keys harder, letting the melody fill the room. The notes run through my brain like miles of too-familiar road. Scenery my eyes no longer see.

It used to be songs would percolate up from deep within, an act of turning myself inside out; but now it's different. Now I can only reach that deep space with paints and brushes and the blackest of charcoal. *February Sea*, beautiful as it is, rings cold. Music has become a means of passing time. It's sad, but that's how life goes. Things change. We adapt.

My fingers send shivers through the piano, running patterns in the upper registers while my brain runs through the day ahead. Richard will retrieve me and scurry me off—not a minute to waste—to Conference Room B for debrief. Then, fashionably late, the Governor will barge into the room with all the bluster of a tornado. Christina will follow, tablet and stylus at the ready. The Governor will bark orders at Richard, who will jump and cough and apologize. The boss will sit and place both hands on the table before moving his gaze over to where I stand behind the second chair to his left. Then he'll smile—I'll see it in his eyes first—and I'll kiss him on the cheek and say, "Hello, Daddy."

The bridge races beneath my fingers, punctuated by accents and trills.

It's always the same. He'll ask about school and I'll tell him what he wants to hear. I'll ask about Mom and he'll do the same. Later, after business is all taken care of, the three of us will travel together over to the stadium and make our appearance at the Patriots' Day celebration. We'll wave, and we'll smile, and we'll leave.

My shoulders slump. I hope Vivian isn't going to be there, too.

Approaching the coda, the music slows, and my fingers press the keys with care, each note growing quieter than the one before. The G arpeggios slow, then stop. My mind hangs blank. I stare at the vase's long shadow, then start again, six measures back, playing low arpeggios into the transition. At the same spot, my fingers stop again.

I stare at my hands, like it's their fault I've forgotten the ending.

How many times have I played this song? I can't remember the next chord, let alone the next note. Suspended sixth? No. Repeat of the bridge? That isn't right either.

The last, wrong chord hangs in the air as my fingers pin the keys in place. The room is so still, even dust motes hang weightless in the window's light.

The floor trembles and the water in the vase ripples. The hanging lights sway. I lift my hands and listen, fingers hovering just above the keyboard.

The floor trembles again and the piano strings whisper a ghostly moan. My foot slips from the sustain pedal. Far across the city, I hear sirens.

Then footsteps. Not Richard's long strides, but hurried, staccato steps. Both doors bang open and two security guys in suits sweep into the room.

"Miss Solomon," the big one says, taking my elbow. The other speaks into his wrist, "Sparrow in the East Room." In a rush of movement, I'm out the door, half carried down fourteen flights of stairs. Fluorescent lights and floor numbers blur past. Twelve. Ten. Seven. Four. By the time the basement bunker doors open, I'm dizzy and my heart pounds a fierce rhythm in my ears.